John Suckling, Frederick A. Strokes

The Poems of Sir John Suckling

with preface and notes

John Suckling, Frederick A. Strokes

The Poems of Sir John Suckling
with preface and notes

ISBN/EAN: 9783337406844

Printed in Europe, USA, Canada, Australia, Japan

Cover: Foto ©Andreas Hilbeck / pixelio.de

More available books at **www.hansebooks.com**

CONTENTS

(FACSIMILE OF SIR JOHN SUCKLING'S SIGNATURE.)

CONTENTS

VERS D' OCCASION.

CHANSONS BACHIQUES.

PREFACE

PREFACE

The fascinating verse of Sir John Suckling, courtier and wit, has not been accessible to the general reader because of the scarcity or high price of the various editions. The present is the only collection of his poems which has been published in this country. Of comparatively recent English editions, that of 1836, with its ponderous memoir by the poet's worthy relative, the Rev. Alfred Suckling, is somewhat scanty, omitting many verses which are given here; while that of 1874, on the contrary, is objectionable because of its retention of many lines and whole poems which are altogether unfit for modern readers, and which do not appear in this volume.

In the garden of Suckling's verse, side by side with rare blossoms of delightful fragrance, grew unsightly and noisome weeds. Of course

they were affected by their surroundings and by
the unnatural light of his court and his time ;
but some of his writings outrage the taste or
morality of to-day.

He is, however, although not as widely
read or known as he should be, one of the
immortals in literature, and had he written nothing but " A Ballad upon a Wedding " and
the song beginning " Why so pale and wan, fond
lover," he would have earned his immortality.
Their simplicity, grace, and wit are unmatched
and are peculiarly his own. Their flavor is most
rare : it delights at once, and is never forgotten.

The path which Suckling's verse takes never
scales sublime heights, but runs through fields
where music and laughter are heard, where
beauty is seen, and where—there are occasional
stormy days. His imagination never awes, nor
does his feeling stir us deeply ; but his fancy
pleases us, his wit and gayety provoke a smile,
and his careless ease and grace charm us.

He conforms thoroughly to the conditions
laid down for the truly successful writer of
vers de société by Frederick Locker, himself a

poet whose lines give us more pleasure than those of any other living writer of " this peculiar species of exquisitely rounded and polished verse." Mr. Locker says: " He must not only be more or less of a poet, but he must, also, be a man of the world, in the most liberal sense of the expression; he must have mixed throughout his life with the most refined and cultivated members of his species, not merely as an idle bystander, but as a busy actor in the throng." Suckling was a poet and a dramatist, a great favorite at the court of Charles I., the intimate of the wits, the reigning belles and beaux, the notables of the day, and was an active participant in affairs of state previous to the execution of Strafford.

Sir John Suckling (also spelled variously, Sutclin, Sutlin, Sutcling, Sutling) was born at Whitton, county of Middlesex, England. The exact date of his birth is not certain; but it is known that he was baptized February 10th, 1608–9.

His parents were noble, and his father filled positions of some dignity under both James I.

and Charles I.   The partial (and somewhat
prolix) Rev. Alfred endeavors to show that the
paternal Suckling, also, was endowed with poetical genius ; but he has slight success in his attempt.   Our poet lost his mother when he was
only five years old, and he succeeded to large
paternal estates at the too early age of eighteen
years.   These facts undoubtedly placed him at
a moral disadvantage and are partly accounta-
ble for some of his misfortunes.

One of his biographers makes the surprising
statement that Suckling "spoke Latin at five
and writ it at nine ;" but it was not until 1623
that he entered Trinity College, Cambridge,
where he distinguished himself in the more
ornamental and polite branches of learning, and
was especially noted for his success in mastering
foreign languages.   His father's death occurred
in the midst of our poet's university career when
valuable possessions in various parts of England
became his,* and in the following year he began

---

*The Rev. Alfred Suckling, " for the amusement of the
ladies," gives a part of the will of the elder Suckling : " I give
to my beloved daughter Martha, a fayre ring, with eleaven

his travels in Germany, France, Italy, and Spain. In Germany, he took an active part in the military operations of Gustavus Adolphus, and acquitted himself with much credit as one of forty sons of gentlemen who served directly under the Marquis of Hamilton, the commander of the English contingent.

In the year 1632, Suckling returned to England, and immediately took the prominent place at the gay and pleasure-loving court to which he was entitled by his gallantry, wit, birth, and wealth. His friend "Will" Davenant (see *Notes*, page 217) says;—"He (Suckling) was famous at court for his accomplishments and readie sparkling witt, that he was the bull that

dyamonds: and to my two pretty twynnes Anne and Mary I give two rings with dyamonds in either of them—viz., to Anne a ring with 13 dyamonds in it, and to Mary one ring with 7 dyamonds in it. Item, I give to my very loving wyfe all her apparell, pearles, rings, and jewelles, which she now weareth, or hath in her possession: save only one chayne of dyamonds, which I lately bought by the help of one Mr. Hardnett, a jeweller, and paid one hundred fifty-five pounds for the same, which is by her to be repayd to my executors within one yeare next after my decease; unless my eldest sonne and she agree about the redemption of the manor of Rose Hall. Item, I give to my well-beloved wyfe my best coach and twoe of my best coach-horses, and she to dwell in my house in Dorset Court (in Fleet Street) soe longe as she remaynes my widdowe."

was bayted; his repartee and witt beinge most sparkling, when most set on and provoked." William Winstanley* says he was, "as the darling of the court."

The young poet plunged deeply into all the frivolity, the recklessness, and the vice of the highest court circles, although he graced his dissipation by many sprightly and polished verses and letters. His entertainments were superb. For some of them he wrote masques which were performed at his house at Whitton†, and for others he devised many original features which now seem quaint. From one of these entertainments—rashly daring youth!—he shut out all ladies "who could not boast of youth and beauty." The Rev. Alfred somewhat naively writes of those who did possess these two graces and were the poet's guests on this occasion: " These ladies Suckling entertained with every rarity which wealth could collect and taste prescribe. But the last course displayed his spright-

---

*Died 1690. Author of *The Lives of the Poets.*

†See *A Prologue to a Masque at Witten* (Page 187), which was written for one of these.

ly gallantry; it consisted not of viands, yet more delicate and choice, but of silk stockings, garters, and gloves, presents at that time of no contemptible value." He is said to have spent hundreds of pounds upon this entertainment, and upon a certain countess "whom he had highly courted, in treating her," some thousands of pounds.

Sir John became distinguished at bowls and cards as well as at rhymes, and the same gossip[*] who tells of the costliness of his courtship of the countess informs us that "no shopkeeper would trust him for sixpence; as to-day, for instance, he might, by winning, be worth £200; the next day, he might not be worth half so much or perhaps sometimes *minus nihilo.*" Mr. Hazlitt has found the following in a newsletter from George Garrard to Lady Conway, 1635: "I heard my Lord Dunhill lost at the Wells at Tunbridge about £2000 at ninepins, most of it to Sir John Sutlin."

When fortune smiled not on Suckling and he lost heavily, Davenant says that, " he would

*John Aubrey, 1626—1697. Antiquarian and writer.

make himself glorious in apparel, and said that it exalted his spirits, and that he had then the best luck when he was most gallant, and his spirits high." The poet himself says (see *A Sessions of the Poets*, page 172) that :—

> " He loved not the Muses, so well as his sport ;
> And prized black eyes or a lucky hit
> At bowls, above all the trophies of wit."

Once, when turning from bowls to black eyes, he met with a sound cudgelling at the hands of a Mr. Digby, "a proper person of great strength and yielded to be the best swordsman of his time," while Aubrey describes Suckling as "of slight strength." After this unlucky experience, " 'twas strange," wrote Aubrey, "to see the evil and ill nature of people, to trample and scoff at, and deject one in disgrace." But Sir John's many brilliant qualities soon enabled him to dispel the clouds of annoyance. At an entertainment of Lady Moray's, when he was undergoing much raillery, his genial hostess called out to him : "' Well ! I am a merrie wench and will never forsake an old friend in disgrace; so, come and sitt downe by me, Sir John.'

Upon this, she seated him at her right hand, and paid him extraordinary attention. Her well-timed kindness raised his dejected spirits so greatly, 'that he threw his repartees about the table with much sparkliness and gentileness of wit, to the admiration of them all.'"

Suckling soon began to devote himself to more serious matters than those which occupied his time during these two or three years after his return from Germany, and he became much engrossed in affairs of state; until, in April, 1635, he was brought before the notice of the dread court of Star Chamber as one of those nobles who disregarded the law compelling them to spend time and money upon their country estates. He speedily withdrew from London and the court, and it was then that he produced most of his best literary work. He lived luxuriously, entertained handsomely, and devoted many of his hours to the Muses, but not for many years; as the troubles of the time (1639) soon drew his attention, and he became again actively engaged in public affairs.

When Charles raised his army to march against the Covenanters, the poet came for-

ward with a princely gift to his monarch in
the shape of a troop of horse which cost the
giver twelve thousand pounds. His horsemen
were picked men, finely equipped and gayly uni-
formed, and were spoken of as the " finest sight"
in the king's forces. In a letter written at the
River Tweed before the enemy had been seen
Suckling describes himself and his fellow soldiers
as " walking up and down like the Tower lions
in their cages ; leaving the people to think what
we would do if we were let loose. The enemy
is not yet much visible ; it may be it is the fault
of the climate, which brings men as slowly for-
ward as plants. But it gives us fears that the
men of peace will draw all to a dumb show, and
so destroy a handsome opportunity, which was
now offered of producing glorious matter for
future chronicle."

Alas ! the "glorious matter" was but an in-
glorious flight of all the king's horses
and all the king's men, including Suckling's
one hundred, red plumes and all. This
was made the occasion of the broadly humorous ballad of Sir John Mennis (see *Notes*,
page 210) which ridiculed the poet —a rival of

the lampooner for literary honors !—and which became a popular song with the Roundheads.

But Suckling's bravery can no more be questioned than that of all other individuals in an army that fled as a body at the first sight of the uncouth, poverty-stricken Scots of Dunse, frenzied, almost, by their deep feeling. Suckling himself says : " Posterity must tell this miracle, that there went an army from the south, of which there was not one man lost nor any man taken prisoner." The incapable—and, perhaps, treacherous—carpet-knight who was Suckling's commander has, indeed, a stain upon his reputation that leaves no whiteness in it ; but no part of the blot can be transferred to the name of the poet for his minor part in the disgraceful fiasco.

And now came the Long Parliament, of which at first our poet was a member, and a keen-sighted and a wise one, until his heart conquered his head, and he became one of the schemers who tried in vain to save the great but venal Strafford from a dire fate. On the fifth of May, 1641, Suckling, with Davenant and others, was summoned for examination by the Parliament as a conspirator against the realm.

He fled across the Channel, and, in Paris, probably in the year 1642, while in his prime, he found a terrible end. Exile, despair, and unaccustomed poverty proved too great a burden, and by his own hand he cast it all off—with his life. Had he lived to return to England and again take up his high position and literary pursuits, his later years might have wonderfully enriched the lyrical verse of our tongue, judging from the fruits of his too-short life.

The portrait of Suckling which has been etched for this edition by Mr. J. S. King is after the painting by Vandyke. The poet is said to have been "of the middle size, though but slightly made; with a winning and graceful carriage and noble features." Aubrey says he was of "brisque eie; his head not very big; his hayre a kind of sand colour; his beard turn'd up naturally, so that he had a brisk and graceful look." He is a thorough Cavalier in appearance, as shown in our portrait of him, and has, certainly, a prepossessing face. He died a bachelor.

After his flight from England several curious

pamphlets directed against him were published, one of which was called "The Sucklington Faction or (Sucklings) Roaring Boyes," testimony to the fact that his enemies had thought him worthy of much notice. The great Milton refers to "Suckling and other conspirators" in connection with an accusation against the king. It is difficult to conceive of a wider difference between two contemporary poets than existed between these. Each in his life and in his writings was a peculiarly fit representative of his own faction—Suckling of the looseness, the wit, the gayety, and the recklessness of the Cavaliers; Milton of the strictness, the lofty thought, the solemnity, and the intensity of purpose of the Parliamentarians.

But in his own true field of light lyrical verse, as Milton in his grander one, our poet stands high and looks down the centuries over the heads of many of his imitators. Many greater poets than himself are accused of appropriation of Suckling's ideas, while Pope took several lines, almost word for word, in his *Essay on Criticism.* Byron, Moore, Leigh Hunt and others are mentioned as "suspects;" while, on the other hand, Suckling in his plays is said to have benefitted by many lines from Shakespeare and Jean de Balzac.

Aside from his poems, little of Sir John Suckling's work is worthy of attention. He wrote four plays, *Aglaura, The Goblins, Brennoralt,* and *The Sad One,* which attracted some attention at court, but whose best features are the songs scattered through them. In these dramatic works, Suckling showed the strong influence which Shakespeare had over him, and he seems to have been an ardent admirer of the great master at a time when the latter was given but meagre attention. Suckling's own lines in *A Supplement of an Imperfect Copy of Verses of Mr. William Shakespeare's* (see page 70 and note upon it) are not altogether unworthy of the author of the *Lucrece.* In one of his letters our poet refers to "my friend, Mr. William Shakespeare," and of this the Rev. Alfred Suckling remarks: "This is probably an expression arising simply from his admiration of our immortal bard; yet he might have seen that writer, while

a boy, and very probably had been in his company."

Many of Suckling's letters are extant, and are
excellent in style, vivacious, and witty; while
some of his serious ones concerning public
affairs show sound judgment and high ability.
But his verses chiefly interest us, and they
alone of his productions are thought worthy of
place in the following pages. The arrangement
which has here been made is wholly different
from that of any previous edition. In fact, this
is the first attempt at grouping together,
under various general headings, such of the
poet's verses as can be so placed with propri-
ety.   F. A. S.

NEW YORK, NOVEMBER, 1886.

SONGS

SONG.

WHY so pale and wan, fond lover?
   Prithee, why so pale?
Will, when looking well can't move her,
   Looking ill prevail?
   Prithee, why so pale?

Why so dull and mute, young sinner?
   Prithee, why so mute?
Will, when speaking well can't win her,
   Saying nothing do 't?
   Prithee, why so mute?

Quit, quit, for shame; this will not move:
   This cannot take her.

If of herself she will not love,

     Nothing can make her:

     The d——l take her!

SONG.

I PRITHEE send me back my heart,
   Since I cannot have thine:
For if from thine thou wilt not part,
   Why then shouldst thou have mine?

Yet now I think on't, let it lie,
   To find it were in vain,
For thou'st a thief in either eye
   Would steal it back again.

Why should two hearts in one breast lie,
   And yet not lodge together?
O love, where is thy sympathy,
   If thus our breasts thou sever?

But love is such a mystery,
   I cannot find it out :
For when I think I'm best resolv'd.
   I then am in most doubt.

Then farewell care, and farewell woe,
   I will no longer pine :
For I'll believe I have her heart,
   As much as she hath mine.

A SONG TO A LUTE.

HAST thou seen the down i' th' air,
      when wanton blasts have toss'd it;
Or the ship on the sea,
      when ruder waves have cross'd it?
Hast thou mark'd the crocodile's weeping,
      or the fox's sleeping?
Or hast view'd the peacock in his pride,
      or the dove by his bride,
      when he courts for his lechery?
O, so fickle, O, so vain, O, so false, so false is she.

THE HONEST LOVER.

HONEST lover whosoever,
    If in all thy love there ever
Was one wav'ring thought, if thy flame
Were not still even, still the same:
        Know this,
        Thou lov'st amiss,
          And, to love true,
Thou must begin again, and love anew.

If, when she appears i'th' room,
Thou dost not quake, and art struck dumb,
And in striving this to cover,
Dost not speak thy words twice over,
        Know this,
        Thou lov'st amiss,

And, to love true,

Thou must begin again, and love anew.

If fondly thou dost not mistake,

And all defects for graces take,

Persuad'st thyself that jests are broken,

When she hath little or nothing spoken,

Know this,

Thou lov'st amiss,

And, to love true,

Thou must begin again, and love anew.

If when thou appear'st to be within,

Thou lett'st not men ask and ask again ;

And when thou answer'st, if it be,

To what was ask'd thee, properly,

Know this,

Thou lov'st amiss,

And, to love true,

Thou must begin again, and love anew.

If when thy stomach calls to eat,

Thou cutt'st not fingers 'stead of meat,

And, with much gazing on her face

Dost not rise hungry from the place,

   Know this,

    Thou lov'st amiss,

    And, to love true,

Thou must begin again, and love anew.

If by this thou dost discover

That thou art no perfect lover,

And, desiring to love true,

Thou dost begin to love anew :

   Know this,

    Thou lov'st amiss,

    And, to love true,

Thou must begin again, and love anew.

THE CARELESS LOVER.

NEVER believe me, if I love,
  Or know what 'tis, or mean to prove;
And yet, in faith, I lie; I do;
And she's extremely handsome too;
    She's fair, she's wondrous fair,
    But I care not who know it,
    Ere I'll die for love, I'll fairly forego it.

This heat of hope, or cold of fear,
My foolish heart could never bear:
One sigh imprisoned ruins more
Than earthquakes have done heretofore:
    She's fair, she's wondrous fair,
    But I care not who know it,
    Ere I'll die for love, I'll fairly forego it.

When I am hungry, I do eat,
And cut no fingers 'stead of meat;
Nor with much gazing on her face
Do e'er rise hungry from the place:
　　　She's fair, she's wondrous fair,
　　　But I care not who know it,
　　　Ere I'll die for love, I'll fairly forego it.

A gentle round fill'd to the brink
To this and t'other friend I drink;
And when 'tis nam'd another's health,
I never make it hers by stealth:
　　　She's fair, she's wondrous fair,
　　　But I care not who know it,
　　　Ere I'll die for love, I'll fairly forego it.

Blackfriars to me, and old Whitehall,
Are even as much as is the fall
Of fountains on a pathless grove,
And nourishes as much my love:
　　　She's fair, she's wondrous fair,

But I care not who know it.

Ere I'll die for love, I'll fairly forego it.

I visit, talk, do business, play,

And for a need laugh out a day:

Who does not thus in Cupid's school,

He makes not love, but plays the fool:

    She's fair, she's wondrous fair,

    But I care not who know it,

    Ere I'll die for love, I'll fairly forego it.

SONG.

THE crafty boy that had full oft essay'd
    To pierce my stubborn and resisting
  breast,
But still the bluntness of his darts betrayed,
Resolv'd at last of setting up his rest.
    Either my wild unruly heart to tame,
    Or quit his godhead, and his bow disclaim.

So all his lovely looks, his pleasing fires,
All his sweet motions, all his taking smiles,
All that awakes, all that inflames desires,
All that by sweet commands, all that beguiles,
    He does into one pair of eyes convey,
    And there begs leave that he himself may
  stay.

And there he brings me, where his ambush lay,

Secure and careless, to a stranger land ;

And never warning me—which was foul play—

Does make me close by all this beauty stand.

    Where first struck dead, I did at last recover,

    To know that I might only live to love her.

So I'll be sworn I do, and do confess,

The blind lad's power, whilst he inhabits there :

But I'll be even with him, nevertheless,

If e'er I chance to meet with him elsewhere.

    If other eyes invite the boy to tarry,

    I'll fly to hers as to a sanctuary.

SONG.

WHEN, dearest, I but think of thee,
    Methinks all things that lovely be
  Are present, and my soul delighted;
For beauties that from worth arise
Are like the grace of deities,
  Still present with us, though unsighted.

Thus whilst I sit, and sigh the day
With all his borrow'd lights away,
  Till night's black wings do overtake me,
Thinking on thee, thy beauties then,
As sudden lights do sleeping men,
  So they by their bright rays awake me.

Thus absence dies, and dying proves
No absence can subsist with loves
    That do partake of fair perfection;
Since in the darkest night they may
By love's quick motion find a way
    To see each other by reflection.

The waving sea can with each flood
Bathe some high promont that hath stood
    Far from the main up in the river:
O, think not then but love can do
As much, for that's an ocean too,
    Which flows not every day, but ever!

PRINCE THERSAMES'S SONG.

NO, no, fair heretic, it needs must be
But an ill love in me,
And worse for thee.

For were it in my power,
To love thee now this hour
More than I did the last;

I would then so fall,
I might not love at all.
Love that can flow, and can admit increase,
Admits as well an ebb, and may grow less.

True love is still the same; the torrid zones,
And those more frigid ones,
It must not know.

For love, grown cold or hot,
> Is lust or friendship, not
> The thing we have.

For that's a flame would die,
Held down or up too high :

> Then think I love more than I can express,
> And would love more, could I but love thee
> less.

SONG.

I PRITHEE spare me, gentle boy,
  Press me no more for that slight toy,
That foolish trifle of an heart ;
I swear it will not do its part,
Though thou dost thine, employ'st thy power
      and art.

For through long custom it has known,
The little secrets, and is grown
Sullen and wise, will have its will,
And, like old hawks, pursues that still
That makes least sport, flies only where't can
      kill.

Some youth that has not made his story,

Will think, perchance, the pain's the glory ;

And mannerly fit out love's feast ;

I shall be carving of the best,

Rudely call for the last course 'fore the rest.

And, O, when once that course is pass'd,

How short a time the feast doth last !

Men rise away, and scarce say grace,

Or civilly once thank the face

That did invite, but seek another place.

SONG.

UNJUST decrees, that do at once exact
    From such a love as worthy hearts should
own,
      So wild a passion,
    And yet so tame a presence
      As holding no proportion,
Changes into impossible obedience.

Let it suffice, that neither I do love
In such a calm observance as to weigh
      Each word I say,
    And each examin'd look t' approve
      That towards her doth move,
      Without so much of fire
As might in time kindle into desire.

Or, give me leave to burst into a flame,
And at the scope of my unbounded will
Love her my fill,
No superscriptions of fame,
Of honour, or good name,
No thought but to improve
The gentle and quick approaches of my love.

But thus to throng and overlade a soul
With love, and then to leave a room for fear,
That shall all that control,
What is it but to rear
Our passions and our hopes on high,
That thence they may descry
The noblest way how to despair and die ?

SONG.

IF you refuse me once, and think again,
    I will complain.
You are deceiv'd ; love is no work of art,
    It must be got and born,
    Not made and worn,
By every one that hath a heart.

Or do you think they more than once can die,
    Whom you deny ?
Who tell you of a thousand deaths a day,
    Like the old poets feign
    And tell the pain
They met, but in the common way.

Or do you think't too soon to yield,
         And quit the field?
Nor is that right, they yield that first entreat;
         Once one may crave for love,
         But more would prove
This heart too little, that too great.

O, that I were all soul, that I might prove
         For you as fit a love,
As you are for an angel; for I know,
None but pure spirits are fit loves for you.

You are all ethereal, there is no dross,
         Nor any part that's gross.
Your coarsest part is like a curious lawn,
The vestal relics for a covering drawn.

Your other parts, part of the purest fire
         That e'er Heaven did inspire;
Makes every thought that is refined by it,
A quintessence of goodness and of wit.

Thus have your raptures reach'd to that degree
         In Love's philosophy,
That you can figure to yourself a fire
Void of all heat, a love without desire.

Nor in Divinity do you go less:
                 You think, and you profess,
That souls may have a plenitude of joy,
Although their bodies meet not to employ.

But I must need confess, I do not find
                 The motions of my mind
So purified as yet, but at the best
My body claims in them an interest.

I hold that perfect joy makes all our parts
                 As joyful as our hearts.
Our senses tell us, if we please not them,
Our love is but a dotage or a dream.

How shall we then agree? you may descend,
   But will not, to my end.
I fain would tune my fancy to your key,
But cannot reach to that obstructed way.

There rests but this, that whilst we sorrow here,
   Our bodies may draw near:
And when no more their joys they can extend,
Then let our souls begin where they did end.

VERS D'OCCASION

A BALLAD.

Upon a Wedding.

I TELL thee, Dick, where I have been,
　Where I the rarest things have seen;
　　O, things without compare!
Such sights again cannot be found
In any place on English ground,
　　Be it at wake or fair.

At Charing-Cross, hard by the way,
Where we (thou know'st) do sell our hay,
　　There is a house with stairs;
And there did I see coming down
Such folks, as are not in our town,
　　Forty at least, in pairs.

Amongst the rest, one pest'lent fine
(His beard no bigger, tho', than thine)
    Walk'd on before the rest :
Our landlord looks like nothing to him :
The King (God bless him) 'twould undo him,
    Should he go still so drest.

At Course-a-Park, without all doubt,
He should have first been taken out
    By all the maids i' th' town :
Though lusty Roger there had been
Or little George upon the Green,
    Or Vincent of the Crown.

But wot you what? the youth was going
To make an end of all his wooing;
    The parson for him staid :
Yet by his leave, for all his haste,
He did not so much wish all past,
    Perchance, as did the maid.

The maid, and thereby hangs a talc,
For such a maid no Whitsun-ale
        Could ever yet produce :
No grape, that's kindly ripe, could be
So round, so plump, so soft as she,
        Nor half so full of juice.

Her finger was so small, the ring
Would not stay on, which they did bring,
        It was too wide a peck :
And to say truth (for out it must)
It looked like the great collar (just)
        About our young colt's neck.

Her feet beneath her petticoat,
Like little mice, stole in and out,
        As if they feared the light :
But O ! she dances such a way !
No sun upon an Easter-day
        Is half so fine a sight.

Her cheeks so rare a white was on,
No daisy makes comparison ;
    Who sees them is undone ;
For streaks of red were mingled there,
Such as are on a Cath'rine pear,
    The side that's next the sun.

Her lips were red, and one was thin,
Compar'd to that was next her chin,
    Some bee had stung it newly ;
But, Dick, her eyes so guard her face ;
I durst no more upon them gaze
    Than on the sun in July.

Her mouth so small, when she does speak,
Thou 'dst swear her teeth her words did break,
    That they might passage get ;
But she so handled still the matter,
They came as good as ours, or better,
    And are not spent a whit.

Passion o'me, how I run on!
There's that that would be thought upon,
    I trow, besides the bride:
The business of the kitchen's great,
For it is fit that men should eat;
    Nor was it there denied.

Just in the nick the cook knocked thrice,
And all the waiters in a trice
    His summons did obey;
Each serving man, with dish in hand,
Marched boldly up, like our train'd band,
    Presented, and away.

When all the meat was on the table,
What man of knife, or teeth, was able
    To stay to be intreated?
And this the very reason was,
Before the parson could say grace,
    The company were seated.

Now hats fly off, and youths carouse ;
Healths first go round, and then the house,
    The bride's come thick and thick :
And when 'twas nam'd another's health,
Perhaps he made it hers by stealth ;
    And who could help it, Dick ?

O' th' sudden up they rise and dance ;
Then sit again, and sigh, and glance ;
    Then dance again and kiss :
Thus several ways the time did pass,
Till every woman wished her place,
    And every man wished his.

By this time all were stol'n aside
To counsel and undress the bride :
    But that he must not know :
But yet 'twas thought he guess'd her mind,
And did not mean to stay behind
    Above an hour or so.

UPON MY LORD BROGHILL'S WED-DING.

DIALOGUE.

S[UCKLING.]   B[OND.]

S. IN bed, dull man,
   When Love and Hymen's revels are
      begun,
And the church ceremonies past and done !

B. Why, who's gone mad to-day?

S. Dull heretic, thou wouldest say,
   He that is gone to heav'n 's gone astray ;
      Broghill our gallant friend
Is gone to church, as martyrs to the fire ;
      Who marry, differ i' th' end,
         Since both do take

The hardest way to what they most desire,

Nor staid he till the formal priest had done,

But ere that part was finish'd, his begun :

Which did reveal

The haste and eagerness men have to seal,

That long to tell the money.

A sprig of willow in his hat he wore

(The lover's badge and liv'ry heretofore),

But now so ordered that it might be taken

By lookers on, forsaking as forsaken.

And now and then

A careless smile broke forth, which spoke his

mind,

And seem'd to say she might have been more

kind.

When this, dear Jack, I saw,

Thought I,

How weak is lovers' law !

The bonds made there like gypsies' knots, with

ease

Are fast and loose, as they that hold them please.

B. But what was the fair nymph's praise or
    power less,
That led him captive now to happiness,
Cause she did not a foreign aid despise,
But enter'd breaches made by others' eyes?

S.   The gods forbid!
There must be some to shoot and batter down,
Others to force and to take in the town.
    To hawks, good Jack, and hearts
              There may
    Be sev'ral ways and arts;
One watches them perchance, and makes them
    tame;
Another, when they are ready, shows them
    game.

TO A LADY THAT FORBADE TO LOVE
BEFORE COMPANY.

WHAT! no more favours? Not a ribbon
more,
Not fan nor muff to hold as heretofore?
Must all the little blisses then be left,
And what was once Love's gift, become our
theft?
May we not look ourselves into a trance,
Teach our souls parley at our eyes, not glance,
Not touch the hand, not by soft wringing there
Whisper a love that only yes can hear?
Not free a sigh, a sigh that's there for you?
Dear, must I love you, and not love you too?
Be wise, nice, fair; for sooner shall they trace
The feather'd choristers from place to place,

By prints they make in th' air, and sooner say

By what right line the last star made his way,

That fled from heaven to earth, than guess to
    know

How our loves first did spring, or how they
    grow.

UPON THE BLACK PATCHES WORN
BY MY LADY D. E.

MADAM:

I KNOW your heart cannot so guilty be,
   That you should wear those spots for
     vanity;
Or as your beauty's trophies, put on one
For ev'ry murder which your eyes have done:
No, they're your mourning-weeds for hearts for-
     lorn
Which, though you must not love, you could not
     scorn;
To whom since cruel honour doth deny
Those joys could only cure their misery;
Yet you this noble way to grace them found,

Whilst thus our grief their martyrdom hath
    crowned.
Of which take heed you prove not prodigal,
For if to every common funeral,
By your eyes martyr'd such grace were allow'd,
Your face should wear not patches, but a cloud.

UPON THE FIRST SIGHT OF MY LADY
SEYMOUR.

WONDER not much, if thus amaz'd I look
    Since I saw you, I have been planet-
  struck:
A beauty, and so rare, I did descry,
As, should I set her forth, you all, as I,
Would lose your hearts likewise; for he that
    can
Know her, and live, he must be more than man.
An apparition of so sweet a creature,
That, credit me, she had not any feature
That did not speak her angel. But no more:
Such heavenly things as these we must adore,
Nor prattle of; lest, when we do but touch,
Or strive to know, we wrong her too—too much.

UPON MY LADY CARLISLE'S WALKING
IN HAMPTON COURT GARDEN.

DIALOGUE.

T[HOMAS C[AREW].   J[OHN] S[UCKLING].

TOM.

DIDST thou not find the place inspir'd,
 And flowers, as if they had desir'd
No other sun, start from their beds,
And for a sight steal out their heads?
Heardst thou not music when she talk'd?
And didst not find that as she walk'd
She threw rare perfumes all about,
Such as bean-blossoms newly out,
Or chafed spices give?——

J. S.

I must confess those perfumes, Tom,
I did not smell; nor found that from
Her passing by ought sprang up new;
The flowers had all their birth from you;
For I passed o'er the self-same walk,
And did not find one single stalk
Of anything that was to bring
This unknown after-after-spring.

TO MY LADY E. C. AT HER GOING OUT
OF ENGLAND.

I MUST confess, when I did part from you,
    I could not force an artificial dew
Upon my cheeks, nor with a gilded phrase
Express how many hundred several ways
My heart was tortur'd, nor with arms across
In discontented garbs set forth my loss :
Such loud expressions many times do come
From lightest hearts: great griefs are always
      dumb.
The shallow rivers roar, the deep are still.
Numbers of painted words may show much
      skill,
But little anguish ; and a cloudy face
Is oft put on, to serve both time and place :

The blazing wood may to the eye seem great,
But 'tis the fire rak'd up that has the heat,
And keeps it long.   True sorrow's like to wine,
That which is good, does never need a sign.
My eyes were channels far too small to be
Conveyers of such floods of misery.
And so pray think, or if you'd entertain
A thought more charitable, suppose some strain
Of sad repentance had, not long before,
Quite emptied for my sins that wat'ry store.
So shall you him oblige that still will be
Your servant to his best ability.

ON NEW-YEAR'S DAY, 1640.

TO THE KING.

AWAKE, great sir, the sun shines here,
    Gives all your subjects a New-Year,
Only we stay till you appear ;
For thus by us your power is understood ;
He may make fair days, you must make them
    good.
        Awake, awake,
        And take
Such presents as poor men can make,
They can add little unto bliss
    Who cannot wish.

May no ill vapour cloud the sky,
Bold storms invade the sovereignty,

But gales of joy, so fresh, so high,

That you may think Heaven sent to try this
year

What sail, or burthen, a king's mind could bear.

Awake, awake,

And take,

Such presents as poor men can make,

They can add little unto bliss

Who cannot wish.

May all the discords in your state

(Like those in music we create),

Be governed at so wise a rate,

That what would of itself sound harsh, or fright,

May be so tempered that it may delight.

Awake, awake,

And take

Such presents as poor men can make,

They can add little unto bliss

Who cannot wish.

What conquerors from battles find,
Or lovers when their doves are kind,
Take up henceforth our master's mind,
Make such strange rapes upon the place, 't may
　　be—
No longer joy there, but an ecstasy.
　　　　Awake, awake,
　　　　And take
　　Such presents as poor men can make,
　　They can add little unto bliss
　　　　Who cannot wish.

May every pleasure and delight,
That has, or does, your sense invite,
Double this year, save those o'th' night;
　　　　Awake, awake,
　　　　And take
　　Such presents as poor men can make,
　　They can add little unto bliss
　　　　Who cannot wish.

TO HIS MUCH HONOURED THE LORD LEPINGTON.

Upon his translation of Malvezzi, his ROMULUS
and TARQUIN.

I T is so rare and new a thing to see
   Ought that belongs to young nobility
In print, but their own clothes, that we must
     praise
You as we would do those first show the ways
To arts or to new worlds. You have begun ;
Taught travell'd youth what 'tis it should have
     done
For 't has indeed too strong a custom been
To carry out more wit than we bring in.

You have done otherwise: brought home, my
    lord,
The choicest things famed countries do afford :
Malvezzi by your means is English grown,
And speaks our tongue as well now as his own.
Malvezzi, he whom 'tis as hard to praise
To merit, as to imitate his ways.
He does not show us Rome great suddenly,
As if the empire were a tympany,
But gives it natural growth, tells how and why
The little body grew so large and high.
Describes each thing so lively that we are
Concerned ourselves before we are aware :
And at the wars they and their neighbours waged,
Each man is present still, and still engag'd.
Like a good perspective he strangely brings
Things distant to us ; and in these two kings
We see what made greatness. ⟨And what 't has
    been
Made that greatness contemptible again.
And all this not tediously derived,

But like to worlds in little maps contrived.
But stay; like one that thinks to bring his friend
A mile or two, and sees the journey's end,
I straggle on too far; long graces do
But keep good stomachs off, that would fall to.

TO HIS FRIEND WILL. DAVENANT.

Upon his Poem of "MADAGASCAR."

WHAT mighty princes poets are! those
        things
The great ones stick at, and our very kings
Lay down, they venture on; and with great ease
Discover, conquer, what and where they please.
Some phlegmatic sea-captain would have staid
For money now, or victuals; not have weighed
Anchor without 'em; thou, Will., dost not stay
So much as for a wind, but go'st away,
Land'st, view'st the country; fight'st, put'st all
        to rout,
Before another could be putting out!
And now the news in town is—Davenant's come
From Madagascar, fraught with laurel home;

And welcome, Will., for the first time; but,
    prithee,
In thy next voyage bring the gold, too, with
    thee.

TO HIS FRIEND WILL. DAVENANT.

Upon his other Poems.

THOU hast redeemed us, Will., and future
    times
Shall not account unto the age's crimes
Dearth of pure wit: since the great lord of it,
Donne, parted hence, no man has ever writ
So near him in 's own way: I would commend
Particulars; but then, how should I end
Without a volume? every line of thine
Would ask, to praise it right, twenty of mine.

TO WILL. DAVENANT.

For Absence.

WONDER not, if I stay here,
    Hurt lovers, like to wounded deer,
Must shift the place; for standing'still
Leaves too much time to know our ill:
Where there is a traitor eye,
That lets in from th' enemy
All that may supplant an heart,
'Tis time the chief should use some art.
Who parts the object from the sense,
Wisely cuts off intelligence.
O, how quickly men must die,
Should they stand all love's battery!
Persinda's eyes great mischief do,
So do we know the cannon too;

But men are safe at distance still :

Where they reach not, they cannot kill.

Love is a fit, and soon is past,

Ill diet only makes it last ;

Who is still looking, gazing ever,

Drinks wine i'th' very height o'th' fever.

SIR JOHN SUCKLING'S ANSWER.

I TELL thee, fellow, whoe'er thou be,
   That made this fine sing-song of me,
      Thou art a rhyming sot ;
These very lines do thee bewray,
This barren wit makes all men say,
      'Twas some rebellious Scot.

But it's no wonder that you sing
Such songs of me, who am no king,
      When every blue cap swears
He 'll not obey King James his ba'rn,
That hugs a bishop under his arm,
      And hangs them in his ears.

Had I been of your covenant,
You would have call'd me John of Gaunt,
    And given me great renown.
But now I am John for the King,
You say I am but a poor Suckling,
    And thus you cry me down.

Well, it's no matter what you say
Of me or mine, that ran away ;
    I hold it no good fashion
A loyal subject's blood to spill,
When we have knaves enough to kill
    By force and proclamation.

Commend me unto Lashly stout,
And all his pedlars him about :
    Tell them without remorse
That I will plunder all their packs
Which they have gotten, with stolen knick-
    knacks,
    With these my hundred horse.

This holy war, this zealous firk,
Against the bishops and the kirk,
    And its pretended bravery—
Religion, all the world can tell,
Amongst Highlanders ne'er did dwell—
    It 's but to cloak your knavery.

Such desperate gamesters as you be,
I cannot blame for tutoring me,
    Since all you have is down ;
And every boor forgets the plough,
And swears that he'll turn gamester now
    And venture for a crown.

UPON SIR JOHN LAURENCE'S BRING-
ING WATER OVER THE HILLS TO
MY L. MIDDLESEX'S HOUSE AT
WITTEN.

A ND is the water come? sure 't cannot be,
It runs too much against philosophy ;
For heavy bodies to the centre bend,
Light bodies only naturally ascend.
How comes this then to pass?   The good
knight's skill
Could nothing do without the water's will:
Then 'twas the water's love that made it
flow,
For love will creep where well it cannot go.

POUR L'AMOUR

PERJURY EXCUSED.

ALAS, it is too late! I can no more
    Love now than I have lov'd before:
My Flora, 'tis my fate, not I;
And what you call contempt, is destiny.
I am no monster, sure, I cannot show
Two hearts; one I already owe;
And I have bound myself with oaths, and vow'd
Oft'ner I fear than Heaven hath e'er allow'd,
That faces now should work no more on me,
Than if they could not charm, or I not see.
And shall I break them? shall I think you can
Love, if I could, so foul a perjur'd man?
O no, 'tis equally impossible that I
Should love again, or you love perjury.

LOVE'S BURNING-GLASS.

WONDERING long, how I could harmless
       see
Men gazing on those beams that fired me ;
At last I found it was the crystal-love
Before my heart, that did the heat improve :
Which, by contracting of those scatter'd rays
Into itself, did so produce my blaze.
Now lighted by my love, I see the same
Beams dazzle those, that me are wont t' inflame.
And now I bless my love, when I do think
By how much I had rather burn than wink.
But how much happier were it thus to burn,
If I had liberty to choose my urn !
But since those beams do promise only fire,
This flame shall purge me of the dross—desire.

THE MIRACLE.

IF thou be'st ice, I do admire
    How thou couldst set my heart on fire;
Or how thy fire could kindle me,
Thou being ice, and not melt thee;
But even my flames, light as thy own,
Have hardened thee into a stone!
Wonder of love, that canst fulfil,
Inverting nature thus, thy will;
Making ice one another burn,
Whilst itself doth harder turn.

A SUPPLEMENT OF AN IMPERFECT COPY OF VERSES OF MR. WILLIAM SHAKESPEARE'S.

By Sir John Suckling.

ONE of her hands one of her cheeks lay
  under,
Cozening the pillow of a lawful kiss,
Which therefore swell'd, and seemed to part
  asunder,
  As angry to be robb'd of such a bliss!
    The one look'd pale and for revenge did
    long,
    While t' other blushed, 'cause it had done
    the wrong.

Out of the bed the other fair hand was
  On a green satin quilt, whose perfect white
Looked like a daisy in a field of grass,
  And showed like unmelt snow unto the sight;
    There lay this pretty perdu, safe to keep
    The rest o'th' body that lay fast asleep.

Her eyes (and therefore it was night), close laid,
  Strove to imprison beauty till the morn:
But yet the doors were of such fine stuff made.
  That it broke through, and show'd itself in
    scorn,
    Throwing a kind of light about the place,
    Which turned to smiles still, as't came near
    her face,

Her beams, which some dull men called hair,
    divided,
  Part with her cheeks, part with her lips did
  sport.
But these, as rude, her breath put by; still some

Wiselier downwards sought, but falling short,
   Curled back in rings, and seem'd to turn
     again
   To bite the part so unkindly held them in.

LOVE'S WORLD.

IN each man's heart that doth begin
　　To love, there 's ever framed within
A little world, for so I found
When first my passion reason drown'd.

EARTH.

Instead of Earth unto this frame,
I had a faith was still the same;
For to be right it doth behove,
It be as that, fixed and not move.

Yet as the Earth may sometimes shake
(For winds shut up will cause a quake),
So often jealousy and fear,
Stol'n into mine, cause tremblings there.

SUN.

My Flora was my Sun ; for as
One Sun, so but one Flora, was ;
All other faces borrow'd hence
Their light and grace, as stars do thence.

MOON.

My hopes I call my Moon ; for they
Inconstant still were at no stay ;
But as my sun inclin'd to me,
Or more or less were sure to be.

Sometimes it would be full, and then
O, too—too soon decrease again ;
Eclips'd sometimes that 'twould so fall
There would appear no hope at all.

STARS AND PLANETS.

My thoughts, 'cause infinite they be,
Must be those many Stars we see ;
Of which some wandered at their will,
But most on her were fixed still.

ELEMENT OF FIRE.

My burning flame and hot desire
Must be the Element of Fire,
Which hath as yet so secret been,
That it, as that, was never seen.

No kitchen fire nor eating flame,
But innocent, hot but in name ;
A fire that's starved when fed, and gone
When too much fuel is laid on.

But, as it plainly doth appear,
That fire subsists by being near
The moon's bright orb ; so I believe
Ours doth, for hope keeps love alive.

AIR.

My fancy was the Air, most free
And full of mutability ;
Big with chimeras, vapours here
Innumerable hatch'd, as there.

SEA.

The Sea's my mind, which calm would be
Were it from winds, my passions, free ;
But out alas ! no Sea I find
Is troubled like a lover's mind.

Within it rocks and shallows be :
Despair and fond credulity.

DAY AND NIGHT.

But in this world it were good reason
We did distinguish time and season ;
Her presence then did make the Day,
And Night shall come when she's away.

WINTER AND SUMMER.

Long absence in far distant place
Creates the Winter ; and the space
She tarried with me, well I might
Call it my Summer of delight.

Diversity of weather came
From what she did, and thence had name ;
Sometimes sh' would smile—that made it fair ;
And when she laughed, the sun shined clear.

Sometimes sh' would frown, and sometimes
     weep,
So clouds and rain their turns do keep ;
Sometimes again sh' would be all ice,
Extremely cold, extremely nice.

But soft, my muse ; the world is wide,
And all at once was not descried :
It may fall out some honest lover
The rest hereafter will discover.

THAT none beguiled be by Time's quick
         flowing,
Lovers have in their hearts a clock still going;
For though Time be nimble, his motions
         Are quicker
         And thicker
    Where Love hath his notions:

Hope is the mainspring on which moves Desire,
And these do the less wheels, Fear, Joy, inspire.
     The balance is Thought, evermore
         Clicking
         And striking,
    And ne'er giving o'er.

Occasion 's the hand which still 's moving round,
Till by it the critical hour may be found,

And when that falls out, it will strike
     Kisses,
     Strange blisses,
And what you best like.

THE INVOCATION.

YE juster powers of Love and Fate,
  Give me the reason why
    A lover cross'd
    And all hopes lost
  May not have leave to die.

It is but just, and Love needs must
Confess it is his part,
    When he doth spy
    One wounded lie,
  To pierce the other's heart.

But yet if he so cruel be
To have one breast to hate,
    If I must live
    And thus survive,
How far more cruel 's Fate?

In this same state I find too late
I am; and here's the grief:
    Cupid can cure,
    Death heal, I'm sure,
Yet neither sends relief.

To live or die, beg only I:
Just Powers, some end me give;
    And traitor-like
    Thus force me not
Without a heart to live.

THE EXPOSTULATION.

TELL me, ye juster deities,
    That pity lovers' miseries,
Why should my own unworthiness
Fright me to seek my happiness?
It is as natural as just
Him for to love, whom needs I must:
All men confess that Love's a fire,
Then who denies it to aspire?

Tell me, if thou wert fortune's thrall,
Wouldst thou not raise thee from the fall?
Seek only to o'erlook thy state,
Whereto thou art condemn'd by fate?
Then let me love my Corydon,

And by Love's leave, him love alone:
For I have read of stories oft,
That Love hath wings, and soars aloft.

Then let me grow in my desire,
Though I be martyr'd in that fire:
For grace it is enough for me,
But only to love such as he:
For never shall my thoughts be base,
Though luckless, yet without disgrace:
Then let him that my love shall blame,
Or clip Love's wings, or quench Love's flame.

DETRACTION EXECRATED.

THOU vermin slander, bred in abject minds
    Of thoughts impure, by vile tongues
    animate,
Canker of conversation ! couldst thou find
Nought but our love whereon to show thy hate ?
Thou never wert when we two were alone ;
What canst thou witness then ? thy base, dull
    aid
Was useless in our conversation,
Where each meant more than could by both be
    said.
Whence hadst thou thy intelligence ; from earth ?
That part of us ne'er knew that we did love :
Or from the air ? Our gentle sighs had birth
From such sweet raptures as to joy did move :

Our thoughts, as pure as the chaste morning's
    breath,
When from the night's cold arms it creeps away,
Were cloth'd in words ; and maiden's blush that
    hath
More purity, more innocence than they.
Nor from the water couldst thou have this tale;
No briny tear hath furrow'd her smooth cheek ?
And I was pleased ; I pray what should he ail
That had her love, for what else could he seek ?
We shorten'd days to moments by love's art,
Whilst our two souls in amorous ecstasy
Perceiv'd no passing time, as if a part
Our love had been of still eternity :
Much less could have it from the purer fire :
Our heat exhales no vapour from coarse sense,
Such as are hopes, or fears, or fond desire ;
Our mutual love itself did recompense.
Thou hast no correspondence had in heaven,
And th' elemental world thou see'st is free :
Whence hadst thou then this talking, monster ?

From hell, a harbour fit for it and thee.

Curs'd be th' officious tongue that did address

Thee to her ears, to ruin my content:

May it one minute taste such happiness,

Deserving lose 't, unpitied it lament!

I must forbear her sight, and so repay

In grief those hours joy shortened to a dram:

Each minute I will lengthen to a day,

And in one year outlive Methusalem.

LOVE'S REPRESENTATION.

L EANING her head upon my breast,
  There on Love's bed she lay to rest;
My panting heart rock'd her asleep,
My heedful eyes the watch did keep;
Then Love by me being harbour'd there,
In Hope to be his harbinger,
Desire his rival kept the door ;
For this of him I begg'd no more,
But that, our mistress t' entertain,
Some pretty fancy he would frame,
And represent it in a dream,
Of which myself should give the theme.
Then first these thoughts I bade him show,
Which only he and I did know,
Array'd in duty and respect,

And not in fancies that reflect,
Then those of value next present,
Approv'd by all the world's consent ;
But to distinguish mine asunder,
Apparell'd they must be in wonder.
Such a device then I would have,
As service, not reward, should crave,
Attir'd in spotless innocence,
Nor self-respect, nor no pretense :
Then such a faith I would have shown,
As heretofore was never known.
Cloth'd with a constant clear intent,
Professing always as it meant.
And if Love no such garments have,
My mind a wardrobe is so brave,
That there sufficient he may see
To clothe Impossibility.
Then beamy fetters he shall find,
By Admiration subt'ly twin'd,
That will keep fast the wanton'st thought,
That e'er imagination wrought :

There he shall find of Joy a chain,

Fram'd by Despair of her disdain,

So curiously that it can't tie

The smallest Hopes that Thoughts now spy.

There Acts, as glorious as the sun,

Are by her veneration spun,

In one of which I would have brought

A pure, unspotted abstract thought.

Considering her as she is good,

Not in her frame of flesh and blood.

These atoms then, all in her sight,

I bade him join, that so he might

Discern between true Love's creation,

And that Love's form that 's now in fashion.

Love granting unto my request

Began to labour in my breast;

But with this motion he did make,

It heav'd so high that she did wake.

Blush'd at the favour she had done,

Then smil'd, and then away did run.

TO MRS. A. L.

THOU think'st I flatter, when thy praise I
tell,
But thou dost all hyperboles excel ;
For I am sure thou art no mortal creature,
But a divine one, thron'd in human feature.
Thy piety is such, that heaven by merit,
If ever any did, thou shouldst inherit.
Thy modesty is such, that hadst thou been
Tempted as Eve, thou wouldst have shunn'd her
sin.
So lovely fair thou art, that sure Dame Nature
Meant thee the pattern of the female creature

Besides all this, thy flowing wit is such,

That were it not in thee, it had been too much

For womankind : should envy look thee o'er,

It would confess thus much, if not much more.

I love thee well, yet wish some bad in thee,

For sure I am thou art too good for me.

UPON TWO SISTERS.

BELIEVE 'T young man, I can as eas'ly tell
   How many yards and inches 'tis to hell;
Unriddle all predestination,
Or the nice points we now dispute upon,
Had the three goddesses been just as fair—

  * * * * * *

It had not been so easily decided,
And sure the apple must have been divided:
It must, it must; he's impudent, dares say
Which is the handsomer till one's away.
And it was necessary it should be so;
While Nature did foresee it, and did know,
When she had fram'd the elder, that each heart
Must at the first sight feel the blind god's dart:
And sure as can be, had she made but one,

No plague had been more sure destruction;
For we had lik'd, lov'd, burnt to ashes too,
In half the time that we are choosing now:
Variety and equal objects make
The busy eye still doubtful which to take;
This lip, this hand, this foot, this eye, this face,
The other's body, gesture, or her grace;
And whilst we thus dispute which of the two,
We unresolv'd go out, and nothing do.
He sure is happiest that has hopes of either,
Next him is he that sees them both together.

TO HIS RIVAL.

NOW we have taught our love to know,
    That it must creep where 't cannot go,
And be for once content to live,
Since here it cannot have to thrive ;
It will not be amiss t' inquire
What fuel should maintain this fire :
For fires do either flame too high,
Or, where they cannot flame, they die.
First then, my half but better heart,
Know this must wholly be her part ;
(For thou and I like clocks are wound
Up to the height, and must move round) :
She then, by still denying what
We fondly crave, shall such a rate
Set on each a trifle, that a kiss

Shall come to be the utmost bliss.

Where sparks and fire do meet with tinder,

Those sparks more fire will still engender :

To make this good, no debt shall be

From service or fidelity ;

For she shall ever pay that score,

By only bidding us do more :

So, though she still a niggard be,

In gracing, where none's due, she's free :

The favours she shall cast on us,

Lest we should grow presumptuous,

Shall not with too much love be shown,

Nor yet the common way still done ;

But ev'ry smile and little glance

Shall look half lent, and half by chance :

The ribbon, fan, or muff that she

Would should be kept by thee or me,

Should not be giv'n before too many,

But neither thrown to' s, when there's any ;

So that herself should doubtful be

Whether 'twere fortune flung 't. or she.

She shall not like the thing we do
Sometimes, and yet shall like it too;
Nor any notice take at all
Of what, we gone, she would extol:
Love she shall feed, but fear to nourish,
For where fear is, Love cannot flourish ;
Yet live it must, nay must and shall,
While Desdemona is at all: '
But when she's gone, then Love shall die,
And in her grave buried lie.

MY dearest rival, lest our love
    Should with eccentric motion move,
Before it learn to go astray,
We'll teach and set it in a way,
And such directions give unto 't,
That it shall never wander foot.
Know first then, we will serve as true
For one poor smile, as we would do,
If we had what our higher flame,
Or our vainer wish, could frame.
Impossible shall be our hope;
And Love shall only have his scope
To join with Fancy now and then,
And think what Reason would condemn:
And on these grounds we'll love as true,
As if they were most sure t' ensue:

And chastely for these things we'll stay,
As if to-morrow were the day.
Meantime we two will teach our hearts
In love's burdens bear their parts :
Thou first shalt sigh, and say she's fair ;
And I'll still answer, "past compare."
Thou shalt set out each part o'th' face,
While I extol each little grace ;
Thou shalt be ravish'd at her wit ;
And I, that she so governs it :
Thou shalt like well that hand, that eye,
That lip, that look, that majesty ;
And in good language them adore :
While I want words and do it more.
Yea, we will sit and sigh awhile,
And with soft thoughts some time beguile
But straight again break out, and praise
All we had done before, new ways.
Thus will we do till paler death
Come with a warrant for our breath,
And then whose fate shall be to die,

First of us two, by legacy
Shall all his store bequeath, and give
His love to him that shall survive ;
For no one stock can ever serve :
To love so much as she'll deserve.

CONTRE L'AMOUR

LOVE AND DEBT ALIKE TROUBLE-
SOME.

THIS one request I make to him that sits
the clouds above,
That I were freely out of debt, as I am out of
love.
Then for to dance, to drink and sing, I should
be very willing,
I should not owe one lass a kiss, nor e'er a
knave a shilling.
'Tis only being in love and debt that breaks us
of our rest ;
And he that is quite out of both, of all the world
is blest :
He sees the golden age, wherein all things were
free and common ;

He eats, he drinks, he takes his rest, he fears no
    man or woman.

Though Crœsus compassed great wealth, yet he
    still craved more,

He was as needy a beggar stiil, as goes from
    door to door.

Though Ovid was a merry man, love ever kept
    him sad ;

He was as far from happiness, as one that is
    stark mad.

Our merchant he in goods is rich, and full of
    gold and treasure ;

But when he thinks upon his debts, that thought
    destroys his pleasure.

Our courtier thinks that he's preferred, whom
    every man envies ;

When love so rumbles in his pate, no sleep
    comes in his eyes.

Our gallant's case is worst of all, he lies so just
    betwixt them ;

For he's in love, and he's in debt, and knows
not which most vex'th him.
But he that can eat beef, and feed on bread
which is so brown
May satisfy his appetite, and owe no man a
crown.

THE CONSTANT LOVER.

[A Poem, with the Answer.]

THE POEM.

Sir J. S.

O^{UT} upon it, I have lov'd
 Three whole days together;
And am like to love three more,
 If it prove fair weather.

Time shall moult away his wings,
 Ere he shall discover
In the whole wide world again
 Such a constant lover.

But the spite on 't is, no praise
    Is due at all to me :
Love with me had made no stays,
    Had it any been but she.

Had it any been but she,
    And that very face,
There had been at least ere this
    A dozen dozen in her place.

The Answer.

SIR TOBY MATTHEWS.

SAY, but did you love so long ?
    In troth, I needs must blame you :
Passion did your judgment wrong,
    Or want of reason shame you.

Truth, Time's fair and witty daughter,
   Shortly shall discover,
Y' are a subject fit for laughter,
   And more fool than lover.

But I grant you merit praise
   For your constant folly:
Since you doted three whole days,
   Were you not melancholy?

She to whom you prov'd so true,
   And that very, very face,
Puts each minute such as you
   A dozen dozen to disgrace.

LOVE TURNED TO HATRED.

I WILL not love one minute more, I swear,
  No, not a minute; not a sigh or tear
Thou gett'st from me, or one kind look again,
Though thou shouldst court me to't and wouldst
     begin.
I will not think of thee, but as men do
Of debts and sins, and then I'll curse thee too:
For thy sake woman shall be now to me
Less welcome, than at midnight ghosts shall
     be:
I'll hate so perfectly, that it shall be
Treason to love that man that loves a she;

Nay, I will hate the very good, I swear,

That's in thy sex, because it doth lie there;

Their very virtue, grace, discourse and wit,

And all for thee; what, wilt thou love me yet?

VERSES.

I AM confirmed a woman can
    Love this, or that, or any other man ;
This day she 's melting hot,
To-morrow swears she knows you not ;
If she but a new object find,
Then straight she 's of another mind.
    Then hang me, ladies, at your door,
    If e'er I doat upon you more.

Yet still I love the fairsome (why ?
For nothing but to please my eye);
And so the fat and soft-skinn'd dame
I 'll flatter to appease my flame ;
For she that's musical I 'll long,

When I am sad, to sing a song.
  Then hang me, ladies, at your door,
  If e'er I doat upon you more.

 I 'll give my fancy leave to range
Through everywhere to find out change ;
The black, the brown, the fair shall be
But objects of variety ;
I 'll court you all to serve my turn,
But with such flames as shall not burn.
  Then hang me, ladies, at your door,
  If e'er I doat upon you more.

THE SIEGE OF A HEART.

'TIS now since I sat down before
    That foolish fort, a heart;
(Time strangely spent!) a year and more,
    And still I did my part:

Made my approaches, from her hand
    Unto her lip did rise,
And did already understand
    The language of her eyes.

Proceeded on with no less art,
    (My tongue was engineer;)
I thought to undermine the heart
    By whispering in the ear.

When this did nothing, I brought down
   Great cannon-oaths, and shot
A thousand thousand to the town,
   And still it yielded not.

I then resolv'd to starve the place
   By cutting off all kisses,
Praying and gazing on her face,
   And all such little blisses.

To draw her out, and from her strength
   I drew all batteries in :
And brought myself to lie at length,
   As if no siege had been.

When I had done what man could do,
   And thought the place mine own,
The enemy lay quiet too,
   And smil'd at all was done.

I sent to know, from whence, and where,
   These hopes and this relief?

A spy informed, Honour was there,
  And did command in chief.

" March, march," quoth I, " the word straight
      give,
  " Let's lose no time, but leave her ;
" That giant upon air will live,
  " And hold it out for ever.

" To such a place our camp remove,
  " As will no siege abide ;
" I hate a fool that starves her love,
  " Only to feed her pride."

LOVING AND BELOVED.

THERE never yet was honest man
  That ever drove the trade of love;
It is impossible, nor can
  Integrity our ends promove;
For kings and lovers are alike in this,
That their chief art in reign dissembling is.

Here we are lov'd, and there we love:
  Good-nature now and passion strive!
Which of the two should be above,
  And laws unto the other give.
So we false fire with arts sometimes discover,
And the true fire with the same art do cover.

What rack can fancy find so high?
   Here we must court, and here engage;
Though in the other place we die.
   O, 'tis torture all, and cozenage!
And which the harder is I cannot tell,
To hide true love, or make false love look well.

Since it is thus, god of desire,
   Give me my honesty again,
And take thy brands back, and thy fire;
   I'm weary of the state I'm in:
Since, if the very best should now befall,
Love's triumph must be Honour's funeral.

THE DISCOMFORT OF LOVE.

IF when Don Cupid's dart
   Doth wound a heart,
      We hide our grief
      And shun relief;
The smart increaseth on that score;
For wounds unsearched but rankle more.

Then if we whine, look pale,
And tell our tale,
      Men are in pain
      For us again;
So neither speaking doth become
The lover's state, nor being dumb.

THE METAMORPHOSIS.

THE little boy, to show his might and
      power,
Turn'd Io to a cow, Narcissus to a flower ;
Transform'd Apollo to a homely swain,
And Jove himself into a golden rain.
These shapes were tolerable, but by the mass
He 's metamorphosed me into an ass.

AGAINST ABSENCE.

MY whining lover, what needs all
    These vows of life monastical?
Despairs, retirements, jealousies,
And subtle sealing up of eyes?
Come, come, be wise; return again,
A finger burnt 's as great a pain;
And the same physic, self-same art
Cures that, would cure a flaming heart,
Wouldst thou, whilst yet the fire is in it,
But hold it to the fire again?
If you, dear sir, the plague have got,
What matter is 't whether or not
They let you in the same house lie,
Or carry you abroad to die?
He whom the plague, or love, once takes,

Every room a pest-house makes.
Absence were good if 't were but sense,
That only holds th' intelligence:
Pure love alone no hurt would do,
But love is love and magic too;
Brings a mistress a thousand miles,
And the sleight of looks beguiles,
Makes her entertain thee there,
And the same time your rival here;
And (O the d—l) that she should
Say finer things now than she would;
So nobly fancy doth supply
What the dull sense lets fall and die.
Beauty, like man's old enemy, is known
To tempt him most when he 's alone:
The air of some wild o'ergrown wood
Or pathless grove is the boy's food.
Return then back, and feed thine eye,
Feed all thy senses, and feast high.
Spare diet is the cause love lasts,
For surfeits sooner kill than fasts.

AGAINST REALIZATION.

FIE upon hearts that burn with mutual fire:
    I hate two minds that breathe but one
    desire:
Were I to curse th' unhallow'd sort of men,
I'd wish them to love, and be lov'd again.
Love's a chameleon, that lives on mere air;
And surfeits when it comes to grosser fare:
'Tis petty jealousies and little fears,
Hopes join'd with doubts, and joys with April
    tears,
That crown our love with pleasures: these are
    gone
When once we come to full fruition.
Like waking in a morning, when all night
Our fancy hath been fed with true delight.

O, what a stroke 'twould be! sure I should die,

Should I but hear my mistress once say ay.

That monster expectation feeds too high

For any woman e'er to satisfy:

Then, fairest mistress, hold the power you have,

By still denying what we still do crave:

In keeping us in hopes strange things to see

That never were, nor are, nor e'er shall be.

NO EXCLUSIVE PROPERTY IN LOVE.

THERE never yet was woman made,
    Nor shall, but to be curs'd,
And O, that I, fond I, should first,
    Of any lover
This truth at my own charge to other fools dis-
    cover!

You that have promised to yourselves
    Propriety in love,
Know women's hearts like straw do move;
    And what we call
Their sympathy, is but love to jet in general.

All mankind are alike to them;
    And though we iron find

That never with a loadstone joined,
    'Tis not the iron's fault,
It is because near the loadstone yet it was never
    brought.

A PLAY AT BARLEY-BREAK.

LOVE, Reason, Hate, did once bespeak
  Three mates to play at barley-break;
Love, Folly took; and Reason, Fancy;
And Hate consorts with Pride; so dance they.
Love coupled last, and so it fell,
That Love and Folly were in hell.

They break, and Love would Reason meet,
But Hate was nimbler on her feet;
Fancy looks for Pride, and thither
Hies, and they two hug together:
Yet this new coupling still doth tell,
That Love and Folly were in hell.

The rest do break again, and Pride
Hath now got Reason on her side;
Hate and Fancy meet, and stand
Untouched by Love in Folly's hand;
Folly was dull, but Love ran well:
So Love and Folly were in hell.

THE GUILTLESS INCONSTANT.

M Y first love, whom all beauties did adorn,
    Firing my heart, suppress'd it with her
    scorn ;
Since like the tinder in my breast it lies,
By every sparkle made a sacrifice.
And now my wand'ring thoughts are not
    confin'd
Unto one woman, but to womankind :
This for her shape I love, that for her face,
This for her gesture, or some other grace :
And so I hope since my first hope is gone,
To find in many what I lost in one ;
And like to merchants after some great loss,
Trade by retail, that cannot do in gross.
The fault is hers that made me go astray,

He needs must wander, that hath lost his way

Guiltless I am; she doth this change provoke,

And made that charcoal, which to her was oak,

And as a looking-glass from the aspect

Whilst it is whole, doth but one face reflect;

But being crack'd or broken, there are grown

Many less faces, where there was but one:

So love unto my heart did first prefer

Her image, and there placed none but her;

But since 't was broke and martyr'd by her
   scorn,

Many less faces in her place are born.

FAREWELL TO LOVE.

WELL-shadow'd landscape, fare ye well :
　　How I have lovèd you, none can tell,
　　At least so well
　　As he that now hates more
　　Than e'er he lov'd before.

But, my dear nothings, take your leave,
No longer must you me deceive,
　　Since I perceive
　　All the deceit, and know
　　Whence the mistake did grow.

As he, whose quicker eye doth trace
A false star shot to a mark'd place,
　　Does run apace,

And thinking it to catch,
A jelly up does snatch

So our dull souls tasting delight
Far off, by sense and appetite
    Think that is right
    And real good ; when yet
    'Tis but the counterfeit.

O, how I glory now, that I
Have made this new discovery!
    Each wanton eye
    Inflamed before: no more
    Will I increase that score.

If I gaze now, 'tis but to see
What manner of death's-head 'twill be,
    When it is free
    From that fresh upper skin,
    The gazer's joy and sin.

The gum and glist'ning which with art
And studied method in each part
  Hangs down the heart,
  Looks (just) as if that day
  Snails there had crawl'd the hay.

The locks, that curl'd o'er each ear be,
Hang like two master-worms to me,
  That, as we see,
  Have tasted to the rest
  Two holes, where they lik'd best.

A quick corse, me-thinks, I spy
In every woman; and mine eye,
  At passing by,
  Checks, and is troubled, just
  As if it rose from dust.

They mortify, not heighten me:
These of my sins the glasses be:

And here I see,
How I have lov'd before,
And so I love no more.

CHANSONS BACHIQUES

CHANSONS BACHIQUES.

I.

A hall, a hall
To welcome our friend :
For some liquor call,
A new or fresh face
Must not alter our pace,
But make us still drink the quicker :
Wine, wine, O, 'tis divine
Come, fill it unto our brother :
What's at the tongue's end,

It forth does send,

And will not a syllable smother.

Then

It unlocks the breast,

And throws out the rest,

And learns us to know each other.

Wine! wine!

II.

Come, let the State stay,

And drink away:

There is no business above it:

It warms the cold brain,

Makes us speak in high strain;

He's a fool that does not approve it.

The Macedon youth

Left behind him this truth,

That nothing is done with much thinking;

He drank and he fought,

Till he had what he sought,
The world was his own by good drinking.

III.

She's pretty to walk with,
And witty to talk with,
And pleasant too to think on:
But the best use of all
Is, her health is a stale
And helps us to make us drink on.

IV.

That box, fair mistress, which thou gav'st to me,
In human guess is like to cost me three,
Three cups of wine and verses six,
The wine will down, but verse for rhyme still
    sticks,
By which you all may easily, gentles, know,
I am a better drinker than a Po—

V.

A CATCH.

Fill it up, fill it up to the brink.
When the pots cry clink,
And the pockets chink,
Then 'tis a merry world.

To the best, to the best, have at her,
And a pox take the woman-hater :—
The Prince of Darkness is a gentleman :
Mahu, Mahu is his name.

VI.

" Some candles here !
And fill us t'other quart, and fill us,
Rogue, drawer, t'other quart.
Some small-beer.
And for the blue,
Give him a cup of sack, 'twill mend his hue."

VII.

Come, come away, to the tavern, I say,
For now at home is washing-day;
Leave your prittle-prattle, let's have a pottle,
We are not so wise as Aristotle.

FRAGMENTS FROM THE
DRAMAS

FRAGMENTS FROM THE DRAMAS.

I.

This moiety war,
  Twilight,
Neither night nor day :
  Pox upon it !
A storm is worth a thousand
  Of your calm ;
There's more variety in it.

II.

Bring them, bring them, bring them in,
See, if they have mortal sin :
Pinch them as you dance about,
Pinch them, till the truth come out.

III.

Welcome, welcome, mortal wight,
To the mansion of the night.
Good or bad, thy life discover;
  Truly all thy deeds declare;
For about thee spirits hover,
  That can tell, tell what they are.
Pinch him, if he speaks not true;
Pinch him, pinch him black and blue.

I.

O, what a day was here! Gently my joys distil.
Lest you should break the vessel you should fill.

SONNETS

SONNETS.

I.

DOST see how unregarded now
    That piece of beauty passes?
There was a time when I did vow
      To that alone;
      But mark the fate of faces;
The red and white works now no more on me,
Than if it could not charm, or I not see.

And yet the face continues good,
      And I have still desires,
And still the self-same flesh and blood,
      As apt to melt,

And suffer from those fires;
O, some kind power unriddle where it lies:
Whether my heart be faulty, or her eyes?

She every day her man does kill,
   And I as often die;
Neither her power then nor my will
     Can question'd be;
   What is the mystery?
Sure beauty's empires, like to greater states,
Have certain periods set, and hidden fates.

II.

OF thee, kind boy, I ask no red and white,
   To make up my delight:
   No odd becoming graces,
Black eyes, or little know-not-whats in faces;
Make me but mad enough, give me good store
Of love for her I court;
   I ask no more,
'Tis love in love that makes the sport.

There's no such thing as that we beauty call,

      It is mere cozenage all ;

      For though some long ago

Lik'd certain colours, mingled so and so,

That doth not tie me now from choosing new :

If I a fancy take

      To black and blue

That fancy doth it beauty make.

'Tis not the meat, but 'tis the appetite

      Makes eating a delight,

      And if I like one dish

More than another, that a pheasant is :

What in our watches, that in us is found ;

So to the height and nick

      We up be wound,

No matter by what hand or trick.

III.

O, FOR some honest lover's ghost,
    Some kind unbodied post

Sent from the shades below!

I strangely long to know,

Whether the nobler chaplets wear,

Those that their mistress' scorn did bear,

Or those that were us'd kindly.

For whatsoe'er they tell us here

To make those sufferings dear,

'Twill there, I fear, be found,

That to the being crown'd

T' have loved alone will not suffice,

Unless we also have been wise,

And have our loves enjoyed.

What posture can we think him in,

That here unloved again

Departs, and's thither gone,

Where each sits by his own?

Or how can that Elysium be,

Where I my mistress still must see

Circled in others' arms?

For there the judges all are just,

    And Sophonisba must

    Be his whom she held dear,

    Not his who loved her here.

The sweet Philoclea, since she died,

Lies by her Pirocles his side,

    Not by Amphialus.

Some bays, perchance, or myrtle bough,

    For difference crowns the brow

    Of those kind souls that were

    The noble martyrs here ;

And if that be the only odds,

(As who can tell ?) ye kinder gods,

    Give me the woman here.

TRANSLATIONS

DESDAIN.

A QUOY servent d'artifices
    Et serments aux vent jettez,
Si vos amours et vos services
    Me sont des importunitez ?

L'amour a d'autres vœux m'appelle ;
    Entendez jamais rien de moy,
Ne pensez nous rendre infidele,
    A me tesmoignant vostre foy.

L'amant qui mon amour possede
    Est trop plein de perfection,
Et doublement il vous excede
    De merit et d'affection.

Je ne puis estre refroidie,
    Ni rompre un cordage si doux,
Ni le rompre sans perfidie,
    Ni d'estre perfidi pour vous.

Vos attentes sont toutes en vain,
    Le vous dire est vous obliger,
Pour vous faire epergner vos peines
    Du vous et du .temps mesnager.

Englished thus by Sir John Suckling.

TO what end serve the promises
        And oaths lost in the air,
Since all your proffer'd services
    To me but tortures are?

Another now enjoys my love,
    Set you your heart at rest:
Think not me from my faith to move,
    Because you faith protest.

The man that does possess my heart,
  Has twice as much perfection,
And does excel you in desert,
  As much as in affection.

I cannot break so sweet a bond,
  Unless I prove untrue :
Nor can I ever be so fond,
  To prove untrue for you.

Your attempts are but in vain
  (To tell you is a favour) :
For things that, may be, rack your brain :
  Then lose not thus your labour.

Εἰ μὲν ἦν μαθεῖν

'Α δεῖ παθεῖν,

Καὶ μὴ παθεῖν,

Καλὸν ἦν τὸ μαθεῖν.

Εἰ δὲ δεῖ παθεῖν

'Α δεῖ μαθεῖν,

Τι δεῖ μαθεῖν;

Χρὴ γὰρ παθεῖν.

Scire si liceret quæ debes subire,

Et non subire, pulchrum est scire:

Sed si subire debes quæ debes scire:

Quorsum vis scire; nam debes subire?

ENGLISHED THUS—

IF man might know
   The ill he must undergo,
And shun it so,
   Then it were good to know :
But if he undergo it,
   Though he know it,
What boots him know it ?
   He must undergo it.

MISCELLANIES

HIS DREAM.

ON a still, silent night, scarce could I num-
  ber
One of the clock, but that a golden slumber
Had locked my senses fast, and carried me
Into a world of blest felicity,
I know not how: first to a garden, where
The apricot, the cherry, and the pear,
The strawberry and plum, were fairer far
Than that eye-pleasing fruit that caused the jar
Betwixt the goddesses, and tempted more
Than fair Atlanta's ball, though gilded o'er.
I gazed awhile on these, and presently
A silver stream ran softly gliding by,
Upon whose banks, lilies more white than snow,

New-fallen from heaven, with violets mixed, did
grow ;
Whose scent so chafed the neighbour-air, that
you
Would softly swear that Arabic spices grew
Not far from thence, or that the place had been
With musk prepar'd, to entertain Love's queen.
Whilst I admired, the river passed away,
And up a grove did spring, green as in May
When April had been moist; upon whose
bushes
The pretty robins, nightingales and thrushes,
Warbled their notes so sweetly, that my ears
Did judge at least the music of the spheres.

AN ANSWER TO SOME VERSES MADE
IN HIS PRAISE.

THE ancient poets and their learned rhymes
    We still admire in these our later times,
And celebrate their fames. Thus, though they
    die,
Their names can never taste mortality:
Blind Homer's muse and Virgil's stately verse,
While any live, shall never need a hearse.
Since then to these such praise was justly due
For what they did, what shall be said to you ?
These had their helps ; they wrote of gods and
    kings,
Of temples, battles, and of such gallant things :
But you of nothing ; how could you have writ,

Had you but chose a subject to your wit?
To praise Achilles or the Trojan crew,
Showed little art, for praise was but their due.
To say she's fair that's fair, this is no pains:
He shows himself most poet, that most feigns:
To find out virtues strangely hid in me;
Ay, there's the art and learned poetry!
To make one striding of a barbed steed,
Prancing a stately round: I use indeed
To ride Bat Jewel's jade; this is the skill,
This shows the poet wants not wit at will.
    I must admire aloof, and for my part
    Be well contented, since you do 't with art.

A POETICAL EPISTLE.

WHETHER these lines do find you out,
    Putting or clearing of a doubt;
Whether predestination,
Or reconciling three in one,
Or the unriddling how men die,
And live at once eternally,
Now take you up—know 'tis decreed
You straight bestride the college steed :
Leave Socinus and the schoolmen,
Which Jack Bond swears do but fool men,
And come to town ; 'tis fit you show
Yourself abroad, that men may know
Whate'er some learned men have guess'd
That oracles are not yet ceas'd :

There you shall find the wit and wine
Flowing alike, and both divine:
Dishes with names not known in books,
And less amongst the college-cooks,
With sauce so pregnant that you need
Not stay till hunger bids you feed.
The sweat of learned Johnson's brain,
And gentle Shakespeare's easier strain,
A hackney-coach conveys you to,
In spite of all that rain can do:
And for your eighteenpence you sit
The lord and judge of all fresh wit.
News in one day as much we 've here,
As serves all Windsor for a year,
And which the carrier brings to you,
After 't has here been found not true.
Then think what company 's design'd
To meet you here, men so refin'd;
Their very common talk at board,
Makes wise or mad a young court-lord,
And makes him capable to be

Umpire in 's father's company.
Where no disputes nor forc'd defence
Of a man's person for his sense
Take up the time; all strive to be
Masters of truth, as victory:
And where you come, I 'd boldly swear
A synod might as easily err.

A SESSIONS OF THE POETS.

A SESSION was held the other day,
    And Apollo himself was at it, they say;
The laurel that had been so long reserv'd,
Was now to be given to him best deserv'd.

                    And

Therefore the wits of the town came thither;
'Twas strange to see how they flock'd together;
Each, strongly confident of his own way,
Thought to gain the laurel away that day.

There was Selden, and he sat hard by the chair;
Weniman not far off, which was very fair;
Sands with Townsend, for they kept no order;
Digby and Shillingsworth a little further.

And

There was Lucan's translator, too, and he

That makes God speak so big in 's poetry;

Selwin and Waller, and Bartlets both the
brothers;

Jack Vaughan and Porter, and divers others.

The first that broke silence was good old Ben,

Prepar'd before with Canary wine,

And he told them plainly he deserv'd the bays,

For his were call'd works, where others were but
plays.

And

Bade them remember how he had purg'd the
stage

Of errors, that had lasted many an age;

And he hoped they did not think the "Silent
Woman,"

The "Fox," and the "Alchemist," out-done by
no man.

Apollo stopped him there, and bade him not go
   on,
'Twas merit, he said, and not presumption,
Must carry 't; at which Ben turned about,
And in great choler offer'd to go out.

                                   But

Those that were there thought it not fit
To discontent so ancient a wit;
And therefore Apollo called him back again,
And made him mine host of his own New Inn.

Tom Carew was next, but he had a fault
That would not well stand with a laureate;
His muse was hard-bound, and th' issue of 's
    brain
Was seldom brought forth but with trouble and
    pain.

                                   And

All that were present there did agree,
A laureate muse should be easy and free,

Yet sure 'twas not that, but 'twas thought that,
    his grace
Considered, he was well he had a cup-bearer's
    place.

Will. Davenant, asham'd of a foolish mischance,
That he had got lately travelling in France,
Modestly hoped the handsomeness of 's muse
Might any deformity about him excuse.

                         And

Surely the company would have been content,
If they could have found any precedent;
But in all their records, either in verse or prose
There was not one laureate without a nose.

To Will. Bartlet sure all the wits meant well,
But first they would see how his snow would
    sell:
Will. smil'd and swore in their judgments they
    went less,
That concluded of merit upon success.

Suddenly taking his place again,
He gave way to Selwin, who straight stepped
    in ;
But, alas! he had been so lately a wit,
That Apollo hardly knew him yet.

Toby Matthews, (pox on him!) how came he
    there ?
Was whispering nothing in somebody's ear ;
When he had the honour to be named in court,
But, sir, you may thank my Lady Carlisle for 't :

For had not her care furnish'd you out
With something of handsome, without all doubt
You and your sorry Lady Muse had been
In the number of those that were not let in.

In haste from the court two or three came in,
And they brought letters, forsooth, from the
    Queen ;

'Twas discreetly done, too, for if th' had come
Without them, th' had scarce been let into the
room.

Suckling next was called, but did not appear;
But straight one whispered Apollo i' th' ear,
That of all men living he cared not for 't,
He loved not the Muses so well as his sport;

And prized black eyes, or a lucky hit
At bowls, above all the trophies of wit;
But Apollo was angry, and publicly said,
'Twere fit that a fine were set upon 's head.

Wat Montague now stood forth to his trial,
And did not so much as suspect a denial;
But witty Apollo asked him first of all,
If he understood his own pastoral.

For, if he could do it, 'twould plainly appear,
He understood more than any man there,

And did merit the bays above all the rest;
But Monsieur was modest, and silence confessed.

During these troubles, in the crowd was hid
One that Apollo soon missed, little Cid;
And having spied him call'd him out of the
    throng,
And advis'd him in his ear not to write so
    strong.

Then Murray was summon'd, but 'twas urg'd
    that he
Was chief already of another company.

Hales set by himself most gravely did smile
To see them about nothing keep such a coil:
Apollo had spied him, but knowing his mind
Passed by, and call'd Falkland that sat just
    behind:
                                        But
He was of late so gone with divinity,

That he had almost forgot his poetry;

Though to say the truth, and Apollo did know
  it,

He might have been both his priest and his poet.

At length who but an Alderman did appear,

At which Will. Davenant began to swear;

But wiser Apollo bade him draw nigher,

And when he was mounted a little higher,

Openly declared that the best sign

Of good store of wit 's to have good store of
  coin;

And, without a syllable more or less said,

He put the laurel on the Alderman's head.

At this all the wits were in such amaze

That for a good while they did nothing but gaze

One upon another; not a man in the place

But had discontent writ in great in his face.

Only the small poets cheer'd up again,
Out of hope, as 'twas thought, of borrowing;
But sure they were out, for he forfeits his crown,
When he lends any poets about the town.

A BARBER.

I AM a barber and, I'd have you know,
   A shaver too, sometimes no mad one
      though :
The reason why you see me now thus bare,
Is 'cause I always trade against the hair.
But yet I keep a state ; who comes to me,
Whosoe'er he is, he must uncover'd be.
When I'm at work, I'm bound to find discourse,
To no great purpose, of great Sweden's force,
Of Witel, and the Bourse, and what 'twill cost
To get that back which was this summer lost.
So fall to praising of his Lordship's hair ;
Ne'er so deform'd, I swear 'tis *sans* compare.
I tell him that the King's doth sit no fuller,

And yet his is not half so good a colour;
Then reach a pleasing glass, that's made to lie,
Like to its master, most notoriously;
And if he must his mistress see that day,
I with a powder send him straight away.}

A PEDLAR OF SMALLWARES.

A PEDLAR I am, that take great care
And mickle pains for to sell smallware:
I had need do so, when women do buy,
That in smallwares trade so unwillingly.

L. W.

A looking-glass, wilt please you, madam, buy?
A rare one 'tis indeed, for in it I
Can show what all the world besides can't do,
A face like to your own, so fair, so true.

L. E.

For you a girdle, madam; but I doubt me
Nature hath order'd there 's no waist about ye;

Pray, therefore, be but pleas'd to search my pack,
There 's no ware that I have that you shall lack

L. B., L. A.

As for you, ladies, there are those behind
Whose ware perchance may better take your
  mind :
One cannot please ye all; the pedlar will draw
  back,
And wish against himself, that you may have
  the knack.

PROLOGUES
AND
EPILOGUES

A PROLOGUE TO A MASQUE AT WITTEN.

EXPECT not here a curious river fine,
    Our wits are short of that: alas the time!
he neat refined language of the court
7e know not; if we did, our country sport
[ust not be too ambitious; 'tis for kings,
'ot for their subjects, to have such rare things.
esides though, I confess, Parnassus hardly,
et Helicon this summer-time is dry:
'ur wits were at an ebb or very low,
nd, to say troth, I think they cannot flow.
ut yet a gracious influence from you
[ay alter nature in our brow-sick crew.
[ave patience then, we pray, and sit a while
nd, if a laugh be too much, lend a smile,

PROLOGUE TO AGLAURA.

I'VE thought upon 't; and cannot tell which
      way
Aught I can say now should advance the play;
For plays are either good or bad : the good,
If they do beg, beg to be understood;
And, in good faith, that has as bold a sound,
As if a beggar should ask twenty pound.
Men have it not about them :
Then, gentlemen, if rightly understood,
The bad do need less prologue than the good;
For, if it chance the plot be lame or blind,
Ill-cloth'd, deform'd throughout, it needs must
      find
Compassion.   It is a beggar without art,

But it falls out in pennyworths of wit,
As in all bargains else—men ever get
All they can in; will have London measure,
A handful over in their very pleasure.
And now ye have 't, he could not well deny ye,
And I dare swear he 's scarce a saver by ye.

PROLOGUE FOR THE COURT.

(*Aglaura.*)

THOSE common passions, hopes and fears,
        that still,
The poets first, and then the prologues fill,
In this our age : he that writ this, by me
Protests against as modest foolery.
He thinks it an odd thing to be in pain
For nothing else, but to be well again.
Who writes to fear is so : had he not writ,
You ne'er had been the judges of his wit ;
And when he had, did he but then intend
To please himself, he sure might have his end
Without th' expense of hope ; and that he had
That made this play, although the play be bad.

Then, gentlemen, be thrifty, save your dooms
For the next man or the next play that comes;
For smiles are nothing where men do not care,
And frowns as little they need not fear.

TO THE KING.

(*Aglaura.*)

THIS Sir, to them, but unto Majesty
    All he has said before he does deny.
Yet not to Majesty—that were to bring
His fears to be but for the Queen and King,
Not for yourselves; and that he dares not say—
You are his sovereigns another way.
Your souls are princes, and you have as good
A title that way, as ye have by blood,
To govern; and here your power's more great
And absolute than in the royal seat.
There men dispute, and but by law obey,
Here is no law at all, but what ye say.

EPILOGUE TO AGLAURA.

OUR play is done, and yours doth now
       begin :
What different fancies people now are in
How strange and odd a mingle it would make,
If, ere they rise, 'twere possible to take
All votes—
But as when an authentic watch is shown,
Each man winds up and rectifies his own,
So in our very judgments ; first there sits
A grave grand jury on it of town-wits,
And they give up their verdict ; then again
The other jury of the court comes in
(And that's of life and death), for each man
       sees,
That oft condemns, what th' other jury frees.

Some three days hence, the ladies of the town
Will come to have a judgment of their own.
And after them, their servants ; then the city.
For that is modest, and is still last witty.
'Twill be a week at least yet, ere they have
Resolv'd to let it live, or give 't a grave.
Such difficulty there is to unite
Opinion, or bring it to be right.

EPILOGUE FOR THE COURT.

(*Aglaura.*)

SIR,

THAT the abusing of your ear 's a crime,
　　Above th' excuse any six lines in rhyme
Can make, the poet knows : I am but sent
T' intreat he may not be a president,
For he does think, that in this place there be
Many have done 't as much and more than he.
But here 's, he says, the difference of the fates,
He begs a pardon after 't, they, estates.

PROLOGUE TO AGLAURA, PRESENTED

AT THE COURT.

'FORE love, a mighty sessions! and, I fear,
    Though kind last 'sizes, 'twill be now
    severe;
For it is thought, and by judicious men,
Aglaura 'scap'd only by dying then.
But 'twould be vain for me now to endear,
Or speak unto my Lords, the Judges here;
They hold their places by condemning still,
And cannot show at once mercy and skill;
For wit 's so cruel unto wit, that they
Are thought to want, that find not want i' th'
    play.
But, ladies, you who never lik'd a plot,

But where the servant had his mistress got,

And whom to see a lover die it grieves,

Although 'tis in worse language that he lives,

Will like 't, we 're confident, since here will be,

That your sex ever lik'd—variety!

PROLOGUE FOR THE COURT.

(Aglaura, presented at the Court.)

'TIS strange, perchance you 'll think, that
she that died
At Christmas, should at Easter be a bride:
But 'tis a privilege the poets have,
To take the long-since dead out of the grave.
Nor is this all; old heroes asleep
'Twixt marble coverlids, and six feet deep
In earth, they boldly wake, and make them do
All they did living here: sometimes more too.
They give fresh life, reverse and alter fate,
And, yet more bold, Almighty-like create,
And out of nothing, only to defy
Reason and Reason's friend, Philosophy;
Fame, honour, valour: all that 's great or good,

Or is at least 'mongst us so understood—
They give; heav'n 's theirs; no handsome
    woman dies,
But, if they please, is straight some star i' th'
    skies,
But O, how those poor men of metre do
Flatter themselves with that that is not true!
And 'cause they can trim up a little prose,
And spoil it handsomely, vainly suppose
They 're omnipotent, can do all those things
That can be done only by gods and kings!
Of this wild guilt he fain would be thought free
That writ this play, and therefore, sir, by me
He humbly begs you would be pleas'd to know,
Aglaura 's but repriev'd this night; and though
She now appears upon a poet's call,
She 's not to live, unless you say say she shall.

EPILOGUE.

PLAYS are like feasts, and every act should
be
Another course, and still variety:
But, in good faith, provision of wit
Is grown of late so difficult to get
That, do we what we can, we are not able
Without cold meats to furnish out the table.
Who knows but it was needless too? maybe,
'Twas here, as in the coachman's trade; and he
That turns in the least compass shows most art,
Howe'er, the poet hopes, sir, for his part,
You'll like not those so much who show their
skill
In entertainment, as who show their will.

PROLOGUE TO THE GOBLINS.

WIT in a prologue poets justly may
    Style a new imposition on a play.
When Shakespeare, Beaumont, Fletcher, rul'd
    the stage,
There scarce were ten good palates in the age;
More curious cooks than guests; for men would
    eat
Most heartily of any kind of meat.
And then what strange variety! each play
A feast for epicures, and that each day!
But mark, how oddly it is come about,
And how unluckily it now falls out;
The plates are grown higher, number increas'd,
And there wants that which should make up
    the feast;

And yet you're so unconscionable, you'd have
Forsooth of late, that which they never gave ;
Banquets before and after,——
Now pox on him that first good prologue writ,
He left a kind of rent-charge upon wit ;
Which if succeeding poets fail to pay,
They forfeit all their worth ; and that's their
      play :
You've ladies' humours, and you're grown to
      that,
You will not like the man, 'less boots and hat
Be right ; no play, unless the prologue be .
And epilogue writ to curiosity.
Well, gentles, 'tis the grievance of the place,
And pray consider 't, for here 's just the case ;
The richness of the ground is gone and spent,
Men's brains grow barren, and you raise the
      rent.

EPILOGUE TO THE GOBLINS.

AND how, and how?—in faith a pretty plot ;
And smartly carried through, too, was it
not ?
And the devils, how? well;—and the fighting ?
Well too ;——a fool, and 't had been just old
writing.
O, what a monster-wit must that man have,
That could please all which now their twelve-
pence gave !
High characters, cries one, and he would see
Things that ne'er were, nor are, nor e'er will be.
Romance, cry easy souls ; and then they swear
The play 's well-writ, though scarce a good line
's there.

The women—O, if Stephen should be kill'd !
Or miss the lady, how the plot is spill'd !
And into how many pieces a poor play
Is taken still before the second day !
Like a strange beauty newly come to court ;
And to say truth, good faith, 'tis all the sport.
One will like all the ill things in a play,
Another some o' th' good, but the wrong way ;
So that from one poor play there comes to rise
At several tables several comedies.
The ill is only here, that 't may fall out
In plays as faces ; and who goes about
To take asunder, oft destroys (we know)
What all together made a pretty show.

NOTES

NOTES

SONG.—PAGE 3.

This is sung by young Orsames in *Aglaura* (Act IV., Scene I.). Francis Turner Palgrave, who has included this ever-living song in his admirable "Golden Treasury of the Best Songs and Lyrical Poems in the English Language," has given it with the heading "Encouragements to a Lover." Orsames calls it "a little foolish counsel, I gave a friend of mine four or five years ago, when he was falling into a consumption."

"*For thou'st a thief in either eye.*"—PAGE 5.

Thou'st is given th' hast in some of the editions. The former is smoother and the meaning is unmistakeable.

A SONG TO A LUTE.—PAGE 7.

Sung to Florelio by a boy in *The Sad One* (Act IV., Scene III.).

"*I never make it hers by stealth.*"—PAGE 12.

Suckling refers here and in *A Ballad upon a Wedding* to this lover's custom. It was, of course, to really drink the health of that fair one "named" to the drinker by himself "by stealth," while ostensibly drinking to the toast of the company.

PRINCE THERSAMES'S SONG.—PAGE 18.

Sung to Aglaura by "A Singing Boy," (*Aglaura*, Act IV., Scene I.).

Song.—Page 20.

These verses are rich with excellent figures.

A Ballad upon a Wedding.—Page 31.

The version of this famous ballad, which has created one of the world's "familiar quotations," is the same as that accepted by Mr. Locker in his delightful *Lyra Elegantiarum.* Mr. Locker is a critic of nice judgment and unquestionable good taste. He says in connection with this ballad : "This is one of his best poems, and as Leigh Hunt says, ' his fancy is so full of gusto as to border on imagination.' Three stanzas of the poem have been necessarily omitted." In reality six stanzas have been cut from the poem as it originally stood.

It was written upon the occasion of the marriage of Suckling's friend, Roger Boyle (Lord Broghill or Brohall, afterwards Earl of Orrery), and Lady Margaret Howard, daughter of the Earl of Suffolk. There are evidences that it was set to music which was very popular.

John Lawson * wrote of the ballad : "This is really excellent, brisk, humorous, witty, and poetical."

---

* The editor is indebted to the Kerslake edition of 1874 for these comments by Lawson and Wordsworth.

The editor of that edition derived them from an old copy of *Suckling's Works* "purporting to have been formerly in the possession of Wordsworth. All the notes written by the poet himself are initialed *W. W.,* or signed in full, evidently to distinguish them from notes in two other hands, those of George Chalmers and John Lawson; but the authenticity of this MS. matter has (it is right to say) been called in question. The handwriting is very like Wordsworth's, which varied a good deal from time to time; but it certainly was thought that, at

Wordsworth wrote : " I fully concur in Mr. Lawson's criticism, but wish that he had been more explicit. * * * This may safely be pronounced his *opus magnum* ; indeed for grace and simplicity it stands unrivalled in the whole compass of ancient or modern poetry."

" *Where we do sell our hay.*"—PAGE 31.
The Haymarket of London of to-day

" *A house with stairs.*"—PAGE 31.
Said to be Suffolk House, afterwards Northumberland House.

" *The maid, and thereby hangs a tale.*"—PAGE 33.
Wordsworth wrote : " His portraits of female beauty are not so finished as those of Moore and Byron, but they possess greater attraction, because he gives only a glimpse and leaves the rest to fancy."

UPON MY LORD BROGHILL'S WEDDING.—PAGE 37.
This was occasioned by the same event which gave rise to the preceding.

" *To hawks, good Jack, and hearts.*"—PAGE 39.
In the edition of 1874 this line has " harts" instead of " hearts." This destroys the figure ; as the meaning is that some hearts must first be tamed as falcons are ; and then these hearts will seize upon the quarry when directed to it.

JACK BOND, an intimate friend of Suckling's. Little is known of him.

any rate. these remarks, whether by Wordsworth or not, could not be without a certain value."

To a Lady that Forbade to Love before Company.—Page 40.

Cibber, in his *Lives of the Poets*, deems these Suckling's best lines. The Rev. Alfred Suckling remarks, in the edition of 1836, " I can not coincide with him in this criticism."

My Lady D. E.—Page 42.

Conjectured by Mr. Hazlitt to be Dorothy Enion, who married Stanley the poet.

" *May no ill vapour cloud the sky.*
　　Bold storms invade the sovereignty."—Page 49.

: Well might the poet wish this at that time. Within the year sat the " long parliament."

To Lord Lepington upon his Translation of Malvezzi.—Page 52.

Lord Lepington's translation was published about 1637.

To Will. Davenant.—Page 55.

Davenant's Poems, edition 1638, contained this and the preceding as prefatory matter.

Sir John Suckling's Answer.—Page 60.

It is not altogether certain that these are Suckling's verses. They appeared first in the edition of 1874, whose editor found them in *MS. Ashmole.*

They are in reference to the effective verses of Sir John Mennis—effective because directed broadly against a conspicuous supporter of a cause obnoxious to the masses, who passed the ballad noisily from lip to lip. It had little merit, and in this respect it stood on a level with the lines given here.

" *Commend me unto Lashly stout.*" Page 61.

Lashly—Lesly, or Leslie, the general of the victorious Scots at Newburn.

"*If thou be'st ice, I do admire.*" —PAGE 69. *Admire*—wonder.

A SUPPLEMENT OF AN IMPERFECT COPY OF VERSES.—PAGE 70.

The reference is to Shakespeare's *Lucrece*.

The first four lines of the first stanza and the first three of the second paraphrase Shakespeare's lines; but the remaining lines of the poem differ widely from those of *Lucrece*. Suckling has here attempted what would now be thought a most ambitious task (and he has not performed it badly); but ideas concerning Shakespeare were then widely different from those now prevailing.

"*Fright me to seek my happinezs?*"—PAGE 82.

"*Fright me.*" Edn. 1836 has "Light me." The former is undoubtedly correct. "Why should my own unworthiness frighten me from seeking my happiness?"

"*Deserving lose't, unpitied it lament!*"—PAGE 86.

"*Deserving lose't.*" Some editions have "deserving loos'd." Our reading is obviously correct.

UPON TWO SISTERS.—PAGE 92.

Line 6 of this poem is lacking and has never been satisfactorily supplied.

THE CONSTANT LOVER.—PAGE 106.

Found (by "A. D.," conjectured by Mr. Hazlitt to be Alexander Dyce), in an obscure volume of verse of the time of Charles I.

A Play at Barley-break.—Page 126.

Barley-break was a game very popular in Suckling's
time. The origin of its designation is not altogether
certain. It may have been derived from " barle bracks,"
meaning " about the stacks " (of grain) ; as in Scotland
it was played in the fields, one player chasing the others
about the stacks, and each, when caught, assisting to
catch the rest. Or, it may come from " *barley** and
break, i. e., breaking of the *parley*, because after a certain time allowed for settling preliminaries, on a cry
being given, it is the business of one to catch as many
prisoners as he can."

In England the game was participated in by six
people at a time, who were divided into three couples,
each couple being formed of a young man and a young
woman. Each couple had its goal, the central goal
being called " hell," and the latter was apportioned by
lot to the couple who were to "catch" the others, if
they ventured from their goals. The penalties were
kisses.

This game has been frequently referred to by Suckling's contemporaries and by earlier poets.

" *A hall,.a hall.*"—Page 137.

Sung by Grainevert, a cavalier, in *The Tragedy of
Brennoralt* (Act II., Scene I.).

" *Come, let the State stay*"—Page 138.

Sung by Grainevert in the same act and scene.

" *The Macedon Youth*"—Page 138.

Alexander the Great.

*Quoted from Dr. Jamieson, who suggested the first deriva-
tion also.

" *She's pretty to walk with.*"—PAGE 139
Sung by Grainevert, *ibid.*

" *Her health is a stale.*"—PAGE 139.
" *A stale.*" This word is now obsolete. Its
meaning here is " a tempting (toast)," " an allurement."

" *That box, fair mistress, which thou gav'st to*
me."—PAGE 139.
Villanor, a cavalier, (*Brennoralt, Act* II., *Scene* I.) is
urged to do his part in the singing and responds in
this song. The preceding lines of the play are :

Mar. Fine and pathetical ! Come, Villanor.
Vil. What's the matter ?
Mar. Come, your liquor and your stanzas : Lines, lines !
Vil. Of what ?
Mar. Why, of anything your mistress has given you.
Vil. Gentlemen, she never gave me anything but a box
O' th' ear for offering to kiss her once.
Str. Of that box then.
Mar. Ay, ay, that box, of that box !
Vil. Since it must be,
Give me the poison then.   [*Drinks and spits.*

A CATCH.—PAGE 140.
Sung by Nassurat, Pellegrin, (cavaliers of Francelia)
and others in *The Goblins* (Act II., Scene I.). Compare with the following from *King Lear* :

" The Prince of Darkness is a gentleman,
Modo he's call'd and Mahu."

In Samuel Harsnet's " Declaration of Popish impos-
tures," the following appears : " Maho was the chief
devil that had possession of Sarah Williams, but
another of the possessed named Richard Mainy, was
molested by a still more considerable fiend called
Modu." (*Note in Hudson's Edition of* KING LEAR.)

Both Shakespeare's and Suckling's lines are probably founded upon something which was old even in
their times.

"*When the pots cry clink*" —PAGE 140.
Edition of 1836 reads, "*When the poets cry clink.*"

"*Some candles here!*—PAGE 140."
Sung by "a Poet," in *The Goblins* (Act I., Scene I.).

"*Come, come away, to the tavern, I say*"—PAGE 141.
Sung by "Actors" in the *The Sad One.* "Signior
Multicarni, the Poet," takes counsel with them as to a
play which is to be acted. The lines which he speaks,
preceding the verses, are :

"Come, let us have one rouse,* my Joves, in Aristippus,
We shall conceive the better afterwards."

"*This moiety war.*"—PAGE 145.
Only half a war. Spoken by Grainevert in *Brennoralt* (Act IV., Scene I.), complaining of inactivity
in camp, and welcoming prospective fighting.

"*Bring them, bring them, bring them in.*"—PAGE 145.
These lines are sung by Tamoren, "king of the thieves,
disguised in a devil's habit," in *The Goblins* (Act I.,
Scene I.).

"*Welcome, welcome, mortal wight.*"—PAGE 146.
Sung by Peridor, one of the thieves, in *The Goblins*
(Act III.).

"*O what a day was here.*"—PAGE 146.
These are the last lines of *The Goblins* and are spoken
by Orsabrin, "a brother to the Prince."

*Rouse, a bumper.

SONNETS.—PAGE 149.

These three poems have been given under this heading in various editions. Of course, the word *sonnet* in this sense means simply "a short poem" and not a sonnet proper.

"So to the height and nick

We up be wound."—PAGE 151.

What matters it by whose hand or by what artifice we are (like our watches) wound up, if the winding be fully done up to the exactly proper point?

Desdain.—PAGE 157.

The old French given here is exactly as in the edition of 1836.

A POETICAL EPISTLE.—PAGE 169.

" This poetical epistle which has considerable merit, is addressed by Suckling to his learned friend John Hales of Eton; he is mentioned in the *Sessions of the Poets* and was one of the first disciples of Socinus in this kingdom." (*Note in edition of* 1836.)

A SESSIONS OF THE POETS.—PAGE 172.

Wordsworth wrote : " The characters of the poets who appear at the Sessions are drawn with great discrimination, particularly that of the poet Jonson."

Selden.—PAGE 172.

John Selden, "the learned antiquary." Statesman as well, 1584-1654.

Weniman.—PAGE 172,

His works and his name are wholly unknown to us.

Sands.—PAGE 172.

George Sandys, son of Edwin Sandys, theologian and Archbishop of York. Published travels, poems, etc., 1577-1644.

Townsend.—PAGE 172.

Doubtful and of slight importance.

Digby.—PAGE 172.

Possibly Sir Kenelm Digby, 1603-1665.

Shillingsworth.—PAGE 172.

Probably William Chillingworth 1602(?)-1644. No poems of his are extant.

" *Lucan's translator.*"—PAGE 173.

Thomas Hay, 1576-1652.

He that makes God speak so big in's poetry."—PAGE 173.

Impossible to tell to whom this refers. Mr. Hazlitt thinks that it may be Francis Quarles.

Selwin.—PAGE 173.

Unknown.

Waller.—PAGE 173.

Edmund Waller, 1605-1687. Editions 1658 and 1836 have *Walter.* Author of some most charming lyrics. One of the best known is, " *Go, lovely Rose.*"

Bartlets.—PAGE 173.

Unknown.

Vaughan—PAGE 173.

Sir John Vaughan, —— -1674 : An intimate friend of Selden's.

Porter.—PAGE 173.

Thought to be Edmond Porter, who published two works, at least, in the 17th Century.

" *Good old Ben.*"—PAGE 173.

Ben Jonson, 1574-1637, the great dramatist. He was poet laureate at the time that this poem was written, (the year of his death).

" *Prepared before with Canary wine.*"—PAGE 173.

Refers to one of the allowances made him by Charles I., " one terce of Spanish wine yearly."

" *Epicœne or the Silent Woman,*" " *The Fox,*" " *The Alchemist.*"—PAGE 173.

Titles of some of Jonson's plays.

Thomas Carew.—PAGE 174.

1589-1639, succeeded Ben Jonson as poet laureate. Many of his verses have great beauty.

Sir William Davenant.—PAGE 175.

1605-1668, a poet of but small merit whose works are almost wholly forgotten. He wrote *Madagascar* (referred to in Suckling's verses to the author) and several plays and poems. He was one of Suckling's most intimate friends.

Toby Matthews.—PAGE 176.

" The reader will find a long notice of this eccentric character in Walpole's *Anecdotes of Painting.*

His Lordship calls him ' one of those heteroclite animals who finds his place anywhere. His father was Archbishop of York, and he a Jesuit. He was supposed a wit, and believed himself a politician : his works are ridiculous'. Suckling has introduced him in the same manner as he has ' Jack Bond ' and ' Tom Carew,'as an occasional interlocutor with himself in his poems. His 'whispering nothing in somebody's ear,' alludes to a ridiculous habit he had of whispering in company."—(*Note in edition of* 1836).

Wat. Montague.—PAGE 177.

Thought to be the Honourable Walter Montague, author of *The Shepherd's Paradise.*

"*Little Cid.*"—PAGE 178.

Thought by the Rev Alfred Suckling to refer to Sidney Godolphin, 1610–1643. A poet and a loyalist.

Hales.—PAGE 178.

The same to whom the *Poetical Epistle* was addressed. (See page 169, and note, page 215.)

Falkland.—PAGE 178.

Viscount Lucius Cary Falkland, 1610–1643. The well-known loyalist. He was an intimate friend of Suckling.

"*I' intreat he may not be a President.*"—PAGE 195.

President----Precedent.

"*Though kind last 'sizes, 'twill be now severe.*—PAGE 196.

"*Sizes*"—Assizes, *i. e.* at the trial of his former play of *Aglaura.*

"*Things that ne'er were, nor are, nor e'er will be.*—PAGE 203.

Comparison is made with Pope's lines :
" Whoever thinks a faultless piece to see,
Thinks what ne'er was, nor is, nor e'er shall be."

The editor acknowledges his indebtedness to the editions of 1836 and 1874, in connection with his preface and notes.

F. A. S.

UNIFORM IN STYLE AND PRICE, IN
FREDERICK A. STOKES & BROTHER'S SE-
RIES OF DAINTILY BOUND POETICAL WORKS,
ARE :

GEORGE ELIOT'S POEMS.

THE SPANISH GYPSY.

CHARLOTTE BRONTÉ'S POEMS.

THOMAS GRAY'S POEMS.

W. M. THACKERAY'S POEMS.

GOETHE'S FAUST.

HEINE'S BOOK OF SONGS.

LONDON RHYMES, *by Frederick Locker.*

LONDON LYRICS, *by Frederick Locker.*

THE GOLDEN TREASURY, *by F. T.*
    Palgrave.

CHARLES DICKENS' POEMS.

LUCILE, *by Owen Meredith.*

TENNYSON'S LYRICAL POEMS.

SONGS FROM BERANGER, *translated*
    by C. L. Betts.

SONGS OF TOIL, *by Carmen Sylva.*

LYRA ELEGANTIARUM, *Locker.*

THE POEMS OF SIR JOHN SUCK-
    LING.

Each one volume, 16mo, on fine laid paper,
wide margins. (Others in preparation.)

Limp parchment-paper $1.00
New half-cloth, illuminated sides, gilt top.   1.00
Half-calf, new colors 2.00
Limp, imitation seal, round corners, gilt edges 2.50
Limp calf, in box 3.00
Tree-calf, new colors 3.50